At ten o'clock the Lynx had barely opened. The music was low and the lighting dim. It was just as well, Amanda thought, steering Harrison toward the bar. The young detective would need a little time to assimilate her surroundings.

Amanda bought her a Coke and reminded her that although they were on duty, for the first hour or so they were simply observing. Just make like the patrons, she advised.

"Which ones?" Harrison glanced nervously about.

A couple of women on the other side of the room blatantly cruised her, one blowing a kiss.

"Relax," Amanda said as a dark-haired woman in severe boy drag approached.

Casey Randall occupied the next barstool and ordered a drink. "I heard you were here." She cast an amused glance at Harrison, adding, "But Alex didn't mention you'd robbed a cradle on the way."

Conscious of a hostile stare from the barwoman, Amanda pasted a sweet smile on her face and said, "You have two choices Casey. You can cooperate, and Harrison and I will conduct our interviews discreetly and tactfully, or you can ask us to leave and we will return sometime in the next few days with twenty uniformed officers who will close you down and escort everyone to the Station."

"That's a threat."

"No," Amanda said mildly. "It's an investigation."

Second Guess

An Amanda Valentine Mystery

by
Rose Beecham

THE NAIAD PRESS, INC.
1994

Printed in the United States of America on acid-free paper
First Edition

Edited by Katherine V. Forrest
Cover design by Bonnie Liss (Phoenix Graphics)
Typeset by Sandi Stancil

Library of Congress Cataloging-in-Publication Data

Beecham, Rose, 1958–
    Second guess / by Rose Beecham.
        p.   cm.
    ISBN 1-56280-069-8
    1. Women detectives—New Zealand—Fiction.   2. Lesbians—New
Zealand—Fiction.   I. Title.
PR9639.3.B344S43   1994
823—dc20   94-16239
                                                                CIP

1510 - 104 - 5 75

*For Mother and Dad,
who keep a light in the window
for all their children.*

ACKNOWLEDGMENTS

Stories don't write themselves. I thank Katherine V. Forrest for her guidance and careful editing. I am also very grateful to the many people who were generous with time and advice in the Wellington CIB, the Wellington Public Library, the Wellington City Art Gallery and the NZ Prostitutes Collective. As usual, my family and friends showed remarkable tolerance and good humor throughout.

ABOUT THE AUTHOR

Rose Beecham is a pseudonym of Jennifer Fulton, author of *Passion Bay, Saving Grace* and *True Love*. A New Zealander, Jennifer divides her time between two cities — Wellington, NZ, and Melbourne, Australia. The Amanda Valentine series includes *Introducing Amanda Valentine, Second Guess* and forthcoming title *Heroic Couplet*.

Books by Jennifer Fulton

PASSION BAY

SAVING GRACE

TRUE LOVE

As "Rose Beecham"

INTRODUCING AMANDA VALENTINE

SECOND GUESS

CHAPTER ONE

Sybil Knight was rich — a fact which may have softened life's little blows, but had granted no favors in death.

Her body, clad only in a pair of lace panties, lay curled, fetus-like, hands cuffed in front of her. Welts criss-crossed her back in a patchwork of dried blood and bruised flesh. Her fine ash blonde hair was caked with blood and her face was swollen and discolored.

She would have been pretty, Amanda thought. Probably beautiful.

Detective Sergeant Gordon Webley, the scene-of-crime officer, cleared his throat and advised tonelessly, "She was discovered by a cleaner at six this morning, Inspector. The area was sealed at six thirty. No weapon in evidence so far."

"Who owns this place?"

Webley referred to his clipboard. "A Ms. Randall. Mount Victoria address. I've sent a car around for her."

They moved aside to enable David Wong, the police photographer, to set up his lights.

"You're certain this is Sybil Knight?" Amanda asked.

"No formal identification, but one of my officers thinks he recognizes her, and the red Mercedes Benz in the parking lot is registered in her name. I've taken the liberty of calling two additional units to secure the site, ma'am. Under the circumstances, it seemed appropriate."

The circumstances, Amanda thought. Sybil Knight, principal curator of the city's art gallery, daughter of a diplomat, is found dead in the dungeon of a lesbian night club.

Amanda gave an inaudible self-pitying sigh. She had returned to the slow lane for *this*? She surveyed the soundproofed room, taking in the bondage equipment — a padded horse, a leather sling suspended by chunky chains, wooden beams in the shape of an X. Someone had sewn elaborate leather and lace curtains for the single cathedral style window. They seemed oddly in step with a rack of ancient-looking canes and a collection of wall-mounted whips.

Emerging from a group of people gathered in the doorway, Moira McDougall, the chief pathologist,

2

picked her way delicately into the scene, adjusted her gold-rimmed spectacles and fired off rapid instructions to her pale-faced minions. Attired in gabardine pants, turtleneck, lab coat and sensible brogues, her sparrow brown hair short and neatly combed, Moira could easily have passed for a stereotypical librarian or teacher. Amanda knew her as a woman of acerbic wit and exacting professional standards. It was Moira's painstaking forensic work that often made the difference between getting a conviction or watching an offender walk.

As the forensic team unpacked their sampling kits, Moira subjected the scene to her customary three minutes' silent evaluation. She paced the room, gloved hands clasped behind her back, eyes traveling the floor and walls. Then she squatted beside the body, head tilted, as though expecting that the dead woman might suddenly roll over and say something. Turning to Amanda, she commented, "I wonder why the killer brought her here."

"What do you mean?"

Moira removed a small cassette recorder from her coat pocket and opened her personal sampling kit, a box-like steel case lined with delicate instruments and small jars. Her expression was reflective. "It seems unlikely one of the patrons would have left such a calling card."

"You don't think this is some kind of bondage scene gone wrong."

"At a glance, no." Moira adjusted her glasses. "But it's early days."

David Wong adjusted his lights and popped his flash experimentally. Amanda decided to get some air.

The July day was cold, the sky overcast, trees

3

creaking in the wind. After a bizarre heat wave the previous year, Wellington's residents had almost convinced themselves that the climate had changed forever. But while Amanda was ten thousand miles away, on leave of absence in New York, the infamous southerly winds had returned and once again the city was vying for the title of bad weather capital of the world.

The Lynx nightclub occupied a prime harbor position on the corner of Jervois Quay and Harris Street, in the same block as Police Headquarters. Above its narrow entranceway a pink neon Lynx prowled atop a discreetly worded sign that read *Lynx Club Members & Guests Only*. Amanda could recall a brief period of public hysteria when the place opened, its proximity to the children's science museum inflaming a few righteous citizens. But after the initial flurry, the media had lost interest, apparently unable to support the titillating speculation with suitably salacious photographs.

A salt-laden gust of air stung Amanda's cheeks. Pulling her jacket collar up, she wandered into the narrow parking lot that skirted the building. From the street, Sybil Knight's red Mercedes was invisible, parked out of sight at the back entrance. The area was cordoned off, a uniformed officer standing guard. Amanda slipped under the police tape and approached the car. It was impossible to see into it through the heavy dew that had collected on the windows.

Had the killer gone to the club with the dead woman? she wondered. Had they argued over something? Had the crime happened in one of the private rooms above the bar, the killer hiding the body until everyone had gone? The Lynx was a women-only venue. Was the perpetrator a woman?

"Inspector . . ."

Amanda turned to face a young auburn-haired woman clutching a notebook in hands dappled pink and blue from the cold. "Lost your gloves again, Harrison?" she inquired.

Appointed to Amanda's team during the Garbage Dump Killer investigation nearly eighteen months ago, Detective Janine Harrison was earnest and ambitious. In what Amanda gathered was an attempt to be taken very seriously, she wore her hair in a regulation-style bun and her skirt below her knees. Harrison could be depended upon to respond to the slightest teasing with profound blushes.

"Casey Randall's arrived, ma'am. DS Webley is with her." Harrison accompanied Amanda to the entrance of the club, where she commented with a note of chagrin, "I haven't viewed the scene, ma'am."

In the obstinate set of Harrison's mouth, Amanda could almost see herself as a rookie cop light years ago. She could guess what the young detective was thinking: that she was junior, female, and she was being denied an opportunity to prove her mettle because her seniors had some old-fashioned notion of protecting her.

She wanted to reassure her colleague somehow, let her know she was not alone. *I'm looking out for you,* she thought, but she said, "You know how Professor McDougall feels about sightseers. You'll see the photographs, Harrison. Right now I want you to report to DSS Shaw and make a start on door-to-door inquiries in the vicinity. Every building, every floor, every restaurant on Civic Square, cleaners, late night deliveries —"

"— fishermen on the dawn shift." Harrison's eyes flashed.

"I'm relying on you for quality leads," Amanda said firmly.

"Yes, ma'am." Harrison checked her watch. "Shall I take notes for your interview with Ms. Randall before I get started?"

Amanda could not help an inward smile. "By all means, thank you Harrison."

Detective Sergeant Webley was standing in the Lynx's entrance hall, skirted by Uniform Branch officers to whom he was relaying instructions. Beyond them, slouched against the stairwell, was a casually dressed woman somewhere in her thirties. Smoke from the cigarette she held drifted into the short dark brown hair combed back from her forehead. Perhaps sensing Amanda's scrutiny, she glanced up, meeting her gaze and expelling a slow steady stream of smoke.

Amanda approached, extending her identification. "Detective Inspector Valentine," she said formally. "I am sorry to have to call you here in such unpleasant circumstances."

"No one has told me a thing." Casey Randall stubbed her cigarette into a large crystal ashtray perched in an alcove behind her. "Perhaps we could discuss this in my office."

"Of course. Detective Harrison will join us, if you don't mind."

Beckoning Harrison, Amanda followed the club owner up several flights of stairs and along a narrow passageway.

6

The room they entered was a step or two down from the Edwardian-style elegance of the entrance foyer. Small. Tidy. Devoid of character. No photos, no plants, no executive furniture; the wallpaper a faded floral and the stained carpet worn through in several places.

Casey Randall turned on a small radiant heater, her glance flicking without interest to Harrison, who had stationed herself just inside the door. "I take it we're talking about a dead body, Inspector," she drawled softly.

"There has been a killing in your club." Amanda placed a small tape recorder on the corner of the desk. "I need to ask you a few questions on tape, if you don't mind."

"You're going to take down what I say and use it as evidence against me." A humorless laugh.

TV cop shows, Amanda thought. They had a lot to answer for.

Casey Randall rolled up her sleeves and subjected Amanda to a slow, thorough appraisal. Her mouth twitched slightly as if she were amused at some private joke.

Convinced she had just been judged lesbian, single and probably sexually frustrated, Amanda asked, "How long have you owned the Lynx nightclub, Ms. Randall?"

"Three years, and the name is Casey."

"Is anyone else involved . . . partner perhaps?"

"I'm single," Casey commented dryly.

"You don't have a business partner?"

"No." Casey extracted a Zippo from the breast pocket of her shirt and flipped the lid on a cigarette box on her desk. "Smoke, Inspector?"

Amanda shook her head. "What kind of clientele frequents your club?"

"Members and their guests," Casey replied unhelpfully.

This was going to be a long day, Amanda thought. "I understand your club is for women only. Could you tell me what activities take place on the premises?"

Casey drew deeply on her cigarette, her hand trembling very slightly. "My club is licensed to sell liquor and food. Members can hire rooms on the upper floors."

"For sexual activity?" Amanda noted Harrison's eyes widening.

"That's up to them." Casey's tone was increasingly tense, her hostility evident.

Capitalizing a little on this defensiveness, Amanda abruptly switched the direction of her questioning. "Where were you last night, Ms. Randall?"

"I was here, and it's Casey."

"Until what time?"

"We closed at two. Monday night's always quiet. I left at about twenty past, I guess."

"Tell me about your closing procedures, Ms. Randall . . . Casey."

"I check each room, lock up . . . put the money in the safe . . ." She broke off. "Look, I know you have a job to do. But this is my club and someone is dead. At least tell me who it is."

"We don't have formal identification yet." Amanda watched the dark-haired woman closely. "But we believe the victim may be Sybil Knight."

Casey froze. "Sybil —"

"You know Ms. Knight?"

8

Casey crushed the life out of her cigarette. Her face had lost all its color. "She's my best friend."

The new Wellington Central Police Headquarters, a dour concrete fortress right opposite the ritzy architectural award-winning Public Library, was supposedly the most earthquake-proof building in earthquake-prone Wellington, destined, come the Big One, to be the nerve center of a massive civil-defense operation.

Around it, buildings would collapse, roads would fissure, panic would reign. The fancy, publicity-snatching library would be reduced to a pile of overpriced rubble, its fake Nikau Palms uprooted, innocents crushed beneath its pretentious marble columns.

Into this unspeakable carnage, from deep within the unscathed walls of Police Headquarters, would emerge the thin blue line. Law and order would prevail. Those who placed functionality and pragmatism ahead of awards and cocktail parties would finally receive the plaudits they deserved. Arty-farts would be laughing on the other sides of their faces.

At least this was the official view. Police management did not want to hear complaints about ludicrous security measures, glitches in the air-con system, windowless rooms. There was no more budget for the new building, and that included putting mirrors in the bathrooms.

Amanda was the fortunate occupant of an office with a harbor view, attractive modern furniture, designer carpet and an air freshener — fragrant pine — which was regularly refilled by the cleaners, who seemed to think she deserved this favored treatment.

She had barely had time to hang her jacket when the phone rang and she was informed that, in a remarkable reversal of protocol, the Chief was on his way to see her. Moments later there was a perfunctory knock and a sturdy man, with a pipe in one hand and a mug of coffee in the other, strode into her office and instructed her to sit down and divert her phone calls.

Chief Inspector Bailey came straight to the point. "I have Sir George Knight in my office — the victim's father. This is a shocking business Valentine, as I'm sure you will appreciate."

"Sir George —" Amanda was conscious of a sinking sensation as she registered the name.

"— former Ambassador to the United States," the Chief supplied. "Owner of Knight & Wentworth Department Stores. Close personal friend of the Minister of Police."

"I see."

"I sincerely hope you do." The Chief was unblinking. "I have given the Minister my personal assurance that this matter will be handled with the utmost discretion. This establishment — the Lynx — presumably its membership is confidential?"

"That's correct." Amanda recalled Casey Randall's flat refusal, later in their interview, to provide a list of members. Most people had gone home, she had stated, by one o'clock in the morning. Reluctantly she had disgorged the names of a few women who had remained until closing.

The Chief asked, "Was Ms. Knight a member?"

"She was the owner's best friend."

The Chief re-lit his pipe. "We have a problem, Valentine," he said softly. "Sybil Knight was not some dopey kid from the suburbs who got herself into the wrong crowd. She was somebody. Her family are somebodies."

"I don't see how her social status affects my investigation." Amanda chose to be obtuse.

"Use your grey matter, Valentine." The Chief tapped his head lightly. Glancing toward the view, he asked, "What manner of person is this Randall woman?"

"Sir?"

"I'm asking if she's the kind who would deem it her public duty to appear on television making indiscreet disclosures about Ms. Knight and her er . . . private life?"

Amanda swallowed several rashly worded replies. "I think that's unlikely," she observed with a trace of cynicism. "Casey Randall has a business to protect."

"Let us hope that responsibility weighs heavily." The Chief's gaze returned sharply to Amanda's face. "I want a muzzle on this one, Valentine. I want the media handled with kid gloves. Am I understood?"

Amanda could almost hear them baying for blood. "Sir, I can't control what they print."

"Of course you can. I've instructed that young lapdog of yours — Harrison isn't it? — to make the necessary arrangements."

"Arrangements?"

The Chief paused on his way to the door. "For the press conference, Valentine."

CHAPTER TWO

"So there I was..." Amanda licked garlic butter off her fingers. "Up to my neck in microphones and what did they all want to know? Was she a lesbian?"

"Well, was she?" With her tongue, Roseanne chased a strand of spaghetti escaping from her fork.

Amanda surveyed her best friend blandly. "You know I can't discuss that."

"So what did you tell them?"

"I threw them a few juicy details and said we're following strong leads et cetera, and we don't want the killer to have any idea of our progress... Need time to consider a large amount of evidence et cetera ... before they blow the lid."

Roseanne snorted. "I don't think much of your chances."

"I groveled," Amanda pointed out.

Roseanne shoved wisps of fine brown hair into her disintegrating topknot. Her expression was dubious.

"Okay, so I sold myself." Amanda picked dolefully at her salad. "I promised a spill-my-guts personal profile if they were willing to keep the lid on."

"How could you? I thought you were finished with the media."

Amanda emptied a pile of Television New Zealand business cards from her pocket onto the table. "They don't know that."

"You don't think a lesbian did it?" Roseanne lowered her fork abruptly. "I mean that club — the Lynx — it's like, a sex club isn't it?"

Amanda raised her eyebrows. "Is it?"

"I know someone who went a couple of times — she didn't join. They've got these rooms where you can ... you know, for sex. And S/M stuff too. That woman — the owner —"

"Casey Randall," Amanda inserted.

"I wouldn't trust her with my washing," Roseanne hissed.

"You know her?"

"Amanda!" Roseanne's soft gray eyes flashed indignation. "She's the woman Miriama had her affair with, remember?"

"Sure I do." Amanda struggled to recall the details. While she was on leave of absence,

14

Roseanne's relationship had ended. Roseanne had written a series of harrowing letters describing her lover's infatuation with another woman. In the end, the other woman had dumped Miriama anyway.

"I don't think you ever mentioned her name," Amanda said.

Roseanne began to laugh. "I suppose I just called her 'that bitch.' "

Sybil Knight's house was a sprawling Victorian villa perched on Brooklyn Hill. According to Amanda's inquiries so far, Sybil had lived there with Kim Curtis, a woman described variously as her lover, a close friend, or her housemate, depending on who was telling the story.

A patrol car was parked in the cobblestone driveway. Behind it, a chauffeur-driven silver Jaguar bearing diplomatic plates was backing up, apparently departing. After identifying his daughter's body, Sir George Knight must have deemed it his duty to break the news to her lover.

Preparing herself for an unpleasant task, Amanda buttoned her coat and crossed the mossy cobblestones to the front entrance.

Ornate stained glass panels enclosed the door, their floral motifs hinting at a summer splendor that would transform the surrounding gardens. Pausing for a moment in the shadow of the veranda, Amanda surveyed the view from Central Park across the inner city to Mt. Victoria. The suburb of Brooklyn had taken inspiration for its street names and landmarks from New York City, but there the resemblance ended. There was no Greenwich Village, no Statue of Liberty, no pollution and the taxi drivers were polite.

For a moment Amanda indulged herself in a pang of regret. She had only returned to New Zealand a few weeks ago and given that she had been uncertain whether she would return at all, she should hardly be surprised that she was having an angst attack about the direction of her life. It was not that she was sorry to be back, she reflected; in fact she felt relieved. She had missed the green beauty, the clean air, the easy pace of life. She had even missed her father.

A retired cop, Valentine Senior had married a New Zealander a few years after his divorce from Amanda's mother. For a time he and his new bride had lived in a small apartment in Queens, but she grew homesick and to Amanda's surprise, her American father had agreed to emigrate. Nowadays he lived his idea of retirement bliss — in a beach condo north of Wellington — big screen television locked on the sports channel, buxom wife baking scones in the kitchen. When he was not preoccupied with football, he was on the phone to Amanda hassling her for details of her most complex investigations.

The call about Sybil Knight would come at nine tonight, Amanda figured, after he'd read the papers and seen the television reports. She must have been out of her mind to come back, she thought morosely. Why had she changed her mind anyway? After five years' absence, she had yearned to go home to New York, yet once there, she had felt displaced. So much had changed, yet so little. There was a time when she could have resigned herself to the everyday trade-off between the most exhilarating and intolerable aspects of big city living. But now, she no longer wanted to. Thirty four years old, she thought grimly, and she was thinking suburban already.

Sybil's lover was sitting hunched in the bay window of a large room, gazing at the same view Amanda had just admired. A slight stiffening of her shoulders was the only hint that she had heard the duty officer introduce Amanda.

Signaling him to remain for the interview, Amanda removed her coat and pulled up a small cane chair. "Ms. Curtis," she said. "I'm so very sorry."

The face that turned to her was strangely blank, hazel eyes dull and unfocused. Kim Curtis got up and jerkily smoothed her clothes. Of medium height, she wore dark tights beneath an oversized sweater. If the bulky outfit was supposed to disguise her extreme thinness, it failed.

"Can I get you a drink, Inspector?" She padded listlessly to a huge chiffonnier.

Amanda declined with a shake of her head. "I know this is terribly difficult —"

"She was my partner, not my friend," Kim Curtis cut across her in a defiant tone. Pouring herself a cognac, she returned to an easy chair near Amanda. "No one will tell me what happened. I need to know."

"Of course you do," Amanda said gently. "Please trust me, Kim. At the moment we're not sure ourselves. Sybil was murdered. We know that much."

Kim lifted her gaze from her glass. "George made me take some pills," she said. "You'd better ask your questions now, before I fall asleep."

Having picked up her role, Sybil's lover seemed

17

determined to play it consummately. She had last seen Sybil the day she died, she told Amanda. They had met for lunch. This was unusual. Ever since Sybil had been appointed to her new job at the City Gallery, she had worked like a dog.

"But we'd had a fight you see," Kim explained. "That was on Sunday night. She left and didn't come home."

"Where did she stay that night?"

Kim fidgeted. "With Marlene. Dr. Marlene Friedman. That's her therapist."

"Did she do that often . . . sleep at Dr. Friedman's house?"

"Sometimes. I think Sybil saw Marlene as a mother substitute." Kim's voice was strained. Lowering her empty glass to the inlaid table beside her chair, she added, "That was pretty much what our fight was about. I suppose I was feeling threatened."

"By Sybil's therapist?"

"In a way. It was stupid, really. Marlene didn't *do* anything." She stared bleakly toward the window.

"So you saw Sybil for lunch on Monday," Amanda prompted. "What did you talk about?"

"She was upset about the fight. She said she wanted for us to take a holiday . . ." She trailed off, holding back a yawn.

"I know this is hard," Amanda said. "But I need to ask you some questions about your relationship with Sybil."

"It's okay." Kim's voice remained dull and flat. "What would you like to know?"

"Tell me about Sybil. What kind of person was she?"

18

Kim's attention seemed to wander, her eyes drawn to a photo on the mantel above the fireplace — Sybil Knight in a red cocktail dress, her pale hair falling in soft waves past a classic oval face. Deep set blue eyes and a slightly crooked mouth rescued her from cheerleader prettiness. Sybil Knight had been a knockout. "She was exciting," Kim said quietly. "A bit mysterious. I was amazed she was interested in me. I don't think I was her usual type."

"When did you start living together?"

"Four years ago."

Amanda had the impression Kim was holding back something painful. Treading carefully, she said. "You mentioned a change in Sybil . . ."

"Relationships have their rough patches." Kim's face showed her strain. "I don't know what caused it. Suddenly it seemed like something was wrong . . . different. God, I don't know. Sybil was in therapy. I didn't want to push her. I couldn't seem to connect with her anymore."

"When did you notice this?"

Kim made a groggy attempt to tuck her legs beneath her and failing that, turned sideways on her chair, resting her head on the soft arm. "About six months ago. She did some kind of seminar and got involved with a support group of people she met there. Then she started seeing Marlene Friedman every week."

The resentment in her tone was obvious. Amanda thought back to Kim's swift assertion that there was nothing going on between Sybil and Marlene. Did she really believe that? "Do you have any idea what issues Sybil was dealing with in her therapy?" she asked.

"She wouldn't talk about it. I think it was family stuff." Kim swept a hand about her. "See all this . . ."

Amanda glanced about the room. The paintings were originals, the rugs hand-knotted, the furniture a choice collection of antique and contemporary pieces. The effect was the kind designers sought to replicate — homely eclecticism combined with old money.

"Sybil inherited the place from her Aunt," Kim explained. "Her family thought her brother Jonathan should have had it . . . the son and heir. They're like that — traditional. Jonathan came here once when Sybil was out — walked around writing in a notebook. Making an inventory. Eventually he sent a ridiculous note saying he would sue us if we sold anything on the list, as it was his children's inheritance. Sybil was furious. They barely spoke for months." Kim sounded bitter. "Well, they got their way in the end. I think Sybil willed the house back to him."

Amanda felt her interest quicken. "Does Jonathan know that?"

"I don't know. I don't really care about the house. I'd live in a shed if it meant I could have Sybil back." Kim cried softly against her sleeve. "I'm sorry. I don't think I can talk anymore."

"It's okay," Amanda said gently. "We can talk again tomorrow. There's just one more thing . . ." Kim did not look up. "Do you know Casey Randall?"

There was no response.

Amanda touched her subject's shoulder lightly. "Kim, wake up. Do you know Casey Randall?"

Kim lifted her head, dazed. "I hate that woman." Almost immediately, she closed her eyes again.

For a long moment Amanda watched her. In

sleep, Kim Curtis's face was pinched and wan. The lines of anxiety etched into her features had not happened overnight, Amanda guessed. Sybil's lover had been unhappy for quite some time.

CHAPTER THREE

Detective Senior Sergeant Joe Moller was pacing Amanda's office, the remains of a sushi lunch in a carton in his hand.

Amanda's partner during her early years with the Wellington CIB, Joe was a big man whose passion for his wife Mabel's cooking had contributed to some fifty extra pounds he'd once carried. Lately, scared by his doctor, he had been dieting and the fifty pounds had shrunk to twenty. But his wardrobe hadn't caught up yet. His suit hung limply, the pants sagging in the seat.

Tugging at his belt, he asked, "Got a minute?"

Amanda dropped her file box and gathered up her messages. "Can it wait?" she muttered.

"You got nothing to do later, huh?"

Amanda sighed. "It's not the Aro Valley thing, is it?"

"You gotta admit, there's something mighty strange going on," Joe said. "We got a bunch of kids disappeared and the bloody parents don't know what day it is. Friggin' hippies."

"So, hand it over to the Child Protection Team." Amanda knew she sounded niggled. Since her return, an indefinable strain had entered the camaraderie she had once shared with Joe. He seemed different somehow. Older. More cantankerous. They were both dieting, she reminded herself. That could account for something.

"Child Protection don't wanna know about kids they can't find," Joe said.

"So what have we got?" Amanda said. "Hunt the body?"

Joe raised his brows at her flippancy. "You having a bad day?"

"Compared to what?" Amanda glanced at her watch. "Ten minutes and I'm out of here, Joe. So give me the bad news first."

Joe refreshed her memory. It had started with the new Aro St. Primary School Administrator. "The dame checks the roll and finds some kids never show so she calls the truancy officer. This turkey visits the

23

parents and they hand him some crap about head lice and measles and say the kids'll be back at school soon. Months later no trace."

"So the Administrator calls us," Amanda said. "We commit two detectives, and what do we find —"

"The kids just happen to be out of town staying with rellies — every last one of them."

"You don't buy this?"

"Jesus wept, Amanda. Five families, all sending a kid off to some long lost Aunty at the same time. In the middle of the school term! You wanna see these people . . . guilty!" Joe mopped his brow. "I want search warrants."

"On what basis? Do we have a single shred of evidence suggesting foul play?"

"We tried contacting these rellies — got an address for some commune-type place up north. No one up there ever heard of the missing kids. You know what I think." Joe dropped his voice to an urgent whisper. "I think we got one of these um . . . satanic cults."

Amanda took a deep breath. "I am not hearing this." She knew of investigations into cult ritual abuse in the United States, but in New Zealand, where everyone knew everyone else's business, the bizarre did not go unreported for long.

"Yeah, well I thought it was flakesville too, kid," Joe said. "But think about it — they're all breeding like bloody rabbits down there, having their babies at home in some kind of hot tub with half the street watching. Poor little bastards don't know whether they're a boy or a girl. Anything could happen."

"You think children are being sacrificed and buried in back gardens by a bunch of crazies? Cannibalism too, maybe?"

24

"I'm trying to be open-minded here, and what do I get?" Joe griped.

"Let's hold off on the warrants," Amanda said. "I want a door-knock. Maybe we can frighten the truth out of them."

"A door-knock in the Aro Valley." Joe brightened. "What the Vice boys wouldn't give."

"That's cheap, Joe."

He was all but rubbing his hands. "You wanna break it to 'em, or shall I?"

For her afternoon appointment with Sybil's family, Amanda took Harrison off door-to-door and ordered up a blue-and-white. It was amazing how rapidly you could traverse the city with a siren sounding and lights flashing.

In the passenger seat, Harrison, a martyr to car sickness, was less than enthusiastic, bailing out almost before Amanda had halted. Notepad clutched to her heaving chest, she stared distractedly at the lofty red brick houses lining the cul de sac. "Nice neighborhood," she managed.

The Knights lived in rarefied splendor in a cluster of ambassadorial dwellings behind the botanical gardens. For their interview, they presented themselves in a tableau that would have done Norman Rockwell justice. They were a striking-looking family; tall, pale and slender.

Sybil's mother, elegant in a burgundy dress and pearls, occupied a small, brocade two-seater. Her husband and son stood behind her, each with a proprietary hand resting on the sofa back. Their demeanor was one of distant superiority, their placid faces betraying nothing of the shock and grief they must surely be feeling. All three focused on Amanda with steely blue eyes.

They will protect their interests at any cost, Amanda found herself thinking as she carried out the introductions. There is almost nothing they wouldn't do.

Stepping forward, the older of the two men led them into the fray. "George Knight, Inspector." He seemed polished and at ease in his role of scion.

"That's Sir George, actually," the younger man inserted. "And my mother is Lady Knight."

"I think we can dispense with the formalities, Jonathan." George Knight dismissed these social pretensions, explaining, "It's not an hereditary title."

Amanda would never understand the nuances of class and protocol that underpinned the English social order. In New Zealand, titles and honors were bestowed on a yearly basis by the English monarch. Many a prominent citizen could look forward to this recognition in later life — some considerably sooner.

She thought about the Queen's Gallantry Medal hanging on her office wall and could sympathize a little with George Knight. It was embarrassing to be singled out for a royal honor when your closest colleagues went unrecognized.

"Would you care for some refreshment, Inspector Valentine?" Lady Knight subjected her to a single all-encompassing glance, determining, Amanda felt certain, her net worth, social status, and probably her sexuality.

No wonder Sybil had been stunning. Her mother possessed the kind of beauty that defied time and surgeon's knife. Declining the offer of tea, Amanda said, "Thank you for seeing me. I appreciate how difficult this is."

Lady Knight glanced up at the two men beside her. Both wore expressions of polite dismay. "I think your timing is bloody awful," Jonathan Knight blustered. "My mother is deeply shocked. Can't this wait until after my sister's funeral?"

Lady Knight lifted a restraining hand to her son's arm. A slight tension in the corners of her mouth revealed emotion held tightly in check.

"Naturally, we want our daughter's killer brought to justice," Sir George smoothly intervened. "Perhaps we could hear your professional opinion of the situation, Inspector."

That Knight Senior had been a career diplomat certainly showed. His son was less circumspect. "I'd say the situation is all too obvious," Jonathan asserted angrily. "I'm not surprised something like this ended up happening. Sybil was a fool. She was involved in a lifestyle no decent woman should even know about. I warned her about it. I —"

"When did you warn her?" Amanda asked.

"I've been telling her for years. Ever since . . ." His gaze was self-righteous and unwavering. "Since she began associating with undesirables."

"Could you be more specific?" Amanda asked without inflection.

Jonathan glanced toward his mother.

Stiff-backed, the image of cool serenity, Lady Knight declared, "We were all concerned about Sybil. You must understand, my daughter had a sheltered upbringing. She was quite naive in many respects —"

Sir George interrupted. "I think my wife is saying

that Sybil was an easy target for the wrong kind of person. She was always impetuous, even as a small child. Jonathan paid regular visits so that we could keep an eye on things, as it were."

"Really?" Amanda addressed Jonathan. "When was the last time you saw Sybil?"

"A week ago."

"Could you tell me about that?" Amanda said.

Jonathan looked uneasy, but, cued by his mother's faint nod, he dutifully complied. "I usually saw Sybil once a week. We dined out since I wasn't welcome at her home." At Amanda's raised eyebrows, he explained tersely, "It was that woman, Kim Curtis. Let's just say we didn't get on."

Catching a look that passed between Jonathan and his mother, Amanda asked, "How did you feel about your sister's sexuality?"

A clock ticked shamelessly into the ensuing silence. Jonathan Knight's face slowly reddened. Lady Knight answered for him. "We have always tried to be tolerant of Sybil's phases. Like many creative people, she experimented."

Ten years of lesbianism, four of them with the same partner. A lengthy experiment. "When you last saw Sybil, what was your general impression of her, Mr. Knight?"

Jonathan gave this a moment's thought. "Now it's interesting that you ask. There was something wrong. I had a feeling about that. I commented on it to Mother."

"Did you ask Sybil what was wrong?"

He shook his head. "I assumed it was personal. In

28

hindsight, I suppose I should have made more of an effort. There might have been something . . ."

"You did all you could, son," Sir George consoled. "None of us had any control over what happened."

"Normally I would have asked her," Jonathan said stiffly. "But we weren't as close as we'd once been." Beneath the stilted words lay distinct grief.

Capitalizing on this, Amanda said, "Your observations about Sybil are very important to this case, Mr. Knight. As someone close to her all her life, you would notice things friends might not. I'll be honest with you. I think Sybil was murdered by a person she knew."

She paused, glancing from one face to the next, seeking the Knights' responses to this statement. They seemed politely impassive, the notion that they could be under suspicion so inconceivable it had not crossed their minds.

"Chief Inspector Bailey assured me the case would be solved quickly," Sir George digressed. "And with a minimum of press attention."

"We're doing our best," Amanda said dryly. "Unfortunately, the media is not renowned for its sensitivity."

"I'm sure we can count on you to act with discretion." Sir George's pleasant tone held a thread of steel. "Do you have a suspect in mind?"

"It would be premature to comment on that." Not to mention stupid, she thought. Close family and friends often complained that they were the last to hear of police progress in solving the murder of a loved one. It seldom occurred to them that the police were hardly likely to release important details to the people most likely, statistically, to have committed the crime.

"Do I take it we are considered suspects?" Lady Knight said with affronted dignity.

"Only until I can rule you out," Amanda responded briskly, "and that should be quite simple. Perhaps we could begin with a statement from each of you with respect to your whereabouts last night. I'm interested in the hours between one and four this morning."

CHAPTER FOUR

"The alibis sound pretty good," Harrison commented as the blue-and-white descended the steep winding route from the Knights' home to the central business district. "Do you really think we can keep the media quiet?"

"Not for long," Amanda said. "They'll be all over us tomorrow."

"A TV crew followed me when I was asking questions in that bistro by the Gallery," Harrison commented. "The owners had to throw them out."

Amanda halted the police car for a set of lights.

Beyond the windscreen, the sky was grim and swollen with rain, gulls congregating on the wharves in shrill anticipation of an impending storm. A couple of blocks ahead, Amanda could see television vans banked up around the Lynx. "Need a ride home?" she asked Harrison.

Her companion hesitated. "Why don't we get a coffee?"

Amanda all but cringed. She had always made a point of spending some informal time with all her junior officers, finding this helped build loyalty and commitment. But she avoided such contact with Harrison, hoping that over time the young detective would see Amanda for what she was — no paragon — and get over her obvious crush. It hadn't happened and sooner or later she would have to deal with it.

Harrison tried again. "They do fabulous brownies at Castro's."

"Sure." Amanda squared her shoulders. "Sounds great."

They found a car park in Majoribanks Street and walked in silence to Castro's cafe. While Harrison looked over the menu posted on a wall, Amanda called the Station.

Detective Senior Sergeant Austin Shaw was conducting inquiries at the City Gallery, she was told. Pathologist Moira McDougall had left a message. Sybil Knight's estimated time of death was 03:00 hours. The full autopsy was scheduled for late tomorrow, providing Moira with enough time to complete her meticulous sampling.

"Brownie?" Harrison inquired.

Calories, Amanda reminded herself unhappily. She peered at the counter food, hoping to connect with a deep craving for sprout salad. After a year off the force, most of it spent eating junk food, she was carrying an extra stone. Working on the theory that exercise would convert the flab to muscle and her body would once again become a lean fighting machine, she had enrolled with a personal trainer. So far the tough schedule had merely increased her appetite.

"They're fresh." Harrison was bent on sabotage.

Disgusted with herself, Amanda caved in. "I'll have mine with cream." Another workout bites the dust. It could be worse. Harrison could declare undying love.

Amanda darted a glance at her admirer. Catching this, Harrison removed her coat and sat down, blushing beneath her freckles. They both started talking at once, apologized, then their coffee and food arrived. Harrison looked like she was about to throw up.

"Inspector, I have to talk to you," she blurted. "Woman to woman."

Amanda tried to swallow a mouthful of brownie. It stuck in the back of her throat like putty. "Okay," she croaked.

"It's about my work." Harrison's voice sounded thin and false. "I can't concentrate."

Amanda washed the brownie down with some coffee, uncertain whether to feel relieved or confused. Perhaps something else was going on. "What's the problem?"

Harrison spooned sugar into her cup for the second time. She seemed to be hyperventilating. "I . . . er . . . You must know I've fallen in love with you."

Reminding herself that she was a mature adult

and a role model for her junior staff, Amanda refrained from leaping up and running away. "I wondered about that," she admitted.

"I thought it would pass," Harrison cried. "I've had this kind of thing before — crushes on older women."

"It's only natural," Amanda said. "You admire someone, you find them interesting —"

"It's more than that. I can't stop thinking about you. When you went away, I thought I would die. Inspector, I know you're —"

"Harrison." Steering well clear of any discussion about her sexuality, Amanda adopted a no-nonsense tone. "I'm glad you've told me about this and I'll help in any way I can. Have you considered a transfer?"

Harrison shook her head vehemently, hazel eyes bright with emotion.

"It may be better if you don't work with me," Amanda went on.

"Better for whom?"

"For you, Harrison. Better for your career."

"I don't care," Harrison mumbled.

"Well, I do. You're an excellent detective. You have a big future. This will pass in time. Why not make it easier on yourself?"

Harrison met Amanda's eyes. "Do you care about me at all?"

Amanda sighed. "Not in the way you want."

"But you are —"

Amanda raised a silencing hand. "My private life is off-limits, Harrison, and I'll tell you why. It doesn't have to do with hiding in closets, or pretending to be something I'm not. It has to do with my sanity. I have to have some place that is all my own — sacrosanct — otherwise this job would swallow me up."

Harrison consumed her brownie in silence. She asked eventually, "Does that rule out having a relationship with another officer?"

Amanda sipped her coffee. "I guess it does."

"I know your private life is off-limits," Harrison said in a small, determined voice. "But are you with anyone at the moment?"

"As it happens I'm not," Amanda replied. "And that's the way I want it to stay for a while."

"Was there someone . . . in the States?"

Amanda thought about Kelly's grave. "A long time ago, there was."

"It's all over?"

Amanda lowered her head. She could almost feel the weight of Kelly dying in her arms, the warm saturation of her blood. "Yes, it's all over."

Harrison looked utterly despondent. "I wish I were dead," she said.

The storm still hadn't struck when Amanda got home. Locking the garage door and heading down the narrow right-of-way that linked her house to the road, she peered up at a sky the color of pansies, deep bruised purple, a little murky with the smoke from numerous chimneys. Night was closing rapidly, the chill air carrying the sounds of homebound traffic.

As she passed the large bungalow above her place, Amanda heard her neighbors arguing, and hesitated for a moment, listening for any hint of escalation. Once or twice, when she had seen the woman outdoors with her two children, Amanda had watched closely for any signs of injury. But it seemed the pair confined themselves to verbal abuse.

Madam bit her ankle and Amanda snatched the little cat into her arms. After a year with Roseanne *and her dog,* Madam had pain to work through. She seemed to feel she should share this with her owner.

"I was a dirtbag," Amanda whispered in her ear. "I'll make it up to you."

The refrigerator was virtually empty, bar Madam's tuna. For a brief foolish moment, Amanda contemplated returning to Castro's for their all-day breakfast — fluffy waffles, thick real home-cured bacon, maple syrup, rich aromatic coffee. Virtuously she repeated beneath her breath, "I enjoy snacking on fresh fruit."

She switched on her answering machine, consuming a banana and a glass of mineral water as the messages scrolled.

Helen, her personal trainer, the woman with muscle definition in her eyelids. *"You're on four miles a day now, Amanda baby. Breathe through the pain."* Terrific, a near-death experience. She could hardly wait.

Roseanne, an oasis of sanity in a world gone mad. *"If you're there pick up the goddamned phone ... No ... fuck ... damn ... I said I need the probation report. Sorry. That wasn't for you. Christ, this place will drive me to an early grave. Ring me when you get in. Pu-leeze."*

Amanda finished her mineral water, tastebuds stricken, siren voices in her head pleading *coff-ee, coff-eee.* There was a slow steady rumble beyond her window. Thunder. She pulled on a tracksuit, laced her Nikes, donned fingerless leather gloves and poked her head out the back door. The rain was still half an hour away, she guessed. Enough time to pull a muscle or two if she really hauled ass.

Bracing herself, she left her house. The air temperature was about three degrees centigrade, not so bad if it weren't for the wind chill factor. In sensible parts of the world winds of eighty miles an hour were considered mild hurricanes — in Wellington, people described them as a stiff breeze.

The sedate white collar suburb of Hataitai was dark and silent, its residents collected around their television sets after another tough day at the office. The grass squelched beneath her feet, and dogs huddled in their kennels, too cold to bother barking as Amanda pounded past their properties.

Taking a steep road down to the sea, she jogged along Evans' Bay, her breath collecting as mist before her. Ducks lined small grubby Hataitai beach, dug into the sand for protection against the elements. The sea was choppy, the yachts at the Marina bobbing and clanking in their moorings.

Amanda hummed the theme from *Chariots of Fire* as she struggled up the zigzag to Rata Road. At the top, she paused clutching her sides, conscious of a strident meowing behind her. Madam, tail switching, flounced past, and with a quick disdainful look over her shoulder set off on a feline trot. She had taken to following Amanda whenever she left the house, once or twice even stowing away in the car. Insecurity, Amanda guessed. Fear of abandonment. Or was it payback?

It was juvenile to feel smug overtaking a cat, especially going downhill, but Amanda felt a certain grim satisfaction getting in the door first. "Sashimi," she announced as Madam flopped through the catflap moments later. "And don't chuck on the carpet, either."

Leaving a frozen dinner nuking in the microwave, she dragged herself to the bathroom. These days she was almost afraid to look in the mirror. Gone was the "glamour cop" people had once recognized in the street. The present day Amanda Valentine needed a new body, a new car and a sex life.

Wishing she had never started lightening her hair, Amanda shed her tracksuit and examined her bottom half in the mirror. No cellulite, and actual contours where formerly there had been lumps. Relieved, she got into the shower and fantasized about hash browns and cholesterol food.

The four-minute lasagna dinner was kind of rubbery but, according to the packet, was only 380 calories and included over half the daily protein allowance of a normal woman. A normal woman apparently ate less than a cat.

Morosely, Amanda switched on the television and flipped channels. A peculiar masochism made her tune into *The Debby Daley Hour*. It was halfway through and Debby, in 'seventies chic, was interviewing a prominent artist who painted all his figures without heads. Amanda indulged herself in a few minutes of torment over her ex-lover's immaculate form, then switched the channel.

She phoned Roseanne as she watched the world news.

"Sorry about the message," her best friend

apologized. "You just wouldn't believe the afternoon I've had . . . anyway . . ."

"I'm listening," Amanda said. Another "family values" English MP had resigned over a sex scandal.

"It's about Sybil Knight," Roseanne said. "I've got a friend who works in the Gallery. We were talking and she thinks it might have been some guy Sybil worked with."

Amanda found a note pad. "What's your friend's name?"

"She doesn't know I'm talking to you, Amanda. Can't we leave her out of it?"

"Rosy, she'll be interviewed anyway."

Roseanne didn't budge. "The guy's name is Todd Parker-Brown. Sounds like he expected to get Sybil's job. He's been telling everyone she was under-qualified and only got the job because her father donated an enormous amount of money to the Gallery."

"What makes your friend think the guy killed Sybil?"

"They had a row on Monday. My friend heard him say 'I'm going to kill the bitch.' Hey!" Roseanne broke off, "Listen to that! Wow! Maybe it's the Big One."

Amanda lowered the receiver, conscious of an unearthly thudding sound. Her windows lit up as lightning struck. "It's just the storm," she said.

"I'm going to watch." Roseanne sounded ecstatic. "Come on over if you want. I've got some beer in the fridge."

Amanda begged off. "I think I'll get an early night."

She killed the television, locked up and went to

her room. It was cold — she had forgotten to turn on the upstairs heating. Rain pounded the iron roof and the windows rattled. Oddly cheered by the elemental turmoil, Amanda gazed out as sheets of lightning illuminated Evans' Bay.

Nature's rhapsodic whims were what she had missed most about New Zealand, she supposed — the wild beauty that encroached so completely on the senses she'd taken it for granted. Amanda had not expected the disembodiment she'd felt when severed from that connection.

A year ago she had wanted quite desperately to go home, to see American flags and hear American voices, eat bagels and cheesecake, catch up with friends, revisit the world she had run from when Kelly had been killed. But there was no going back. Friends had moved on. Her mother no longer lived in Brooklyn. Was that why New York had seemed so lonely? Or was there an equally mundane explanation for that familiar empty ache — the lack of a steady girlfriend, maybe?

Putting this thought right out of her mind, Amanda undressed and crawled between her chilly sheets, concentrating on the voluptuous assault of wind and rain. At this rate, jogging would be out of the question tomorrow.

CHAPTER FIVE

When the glamorous new Public Library had been built, its former home was offered to the City Gallery. This had caused embarrassment to Gallery officials bent on pursuing a truly South Pacific identity, for the disused library building was a neo-classical monument to 1930s European architecture, a reminder of a colonized past liberals sought to disclaim. All the same, it was large and stately and dominated Civic Square. Some people felt it made the new library look a little cheap.

As a sweetener, the Council had offered an

exciting renovation program and an elevation in status for the Gallery. The new Mayor, Fran Wilde, said she wanted to put Wellington on the cultural map. It was time to bring the contemporary visual arts to the people. After years of neglect by City Councilors who treated the arts as a poor cousin of really important community endeavors such as rugby and car racing, this had caused something of a flutter.

Responding to the challenge, the Gallery had moved, restructured, assessed its priorities, and created an entirely new position for a Principal Curator, a person of vision and reputation who would steer the Gallery's exhibition and publications programs daringly closer to the leading edge. The job had attracted applicants from all over the country as well as overseas.

"I'll be blunt," said Todd Parker-Brown, the third person Amanda and Austin Shaw had interviewed at the Gallery that morning. "They appointed the wrong person."

He was not a particularly appealing man, Amanda thought. He had chosen an after-shave that probably sounded sexy in its advertising but did not work for him. His eyes were a torpid muddy green. Above them dark eyebrows descended toward the narrow bridge of his nose where they were connected by a few straggling hairs. He would pluck these when he was dating, Amanda decided.

She examined the magazine clipping Austin Shaw had handed her as they crossed the road from Police Headquarters to the Gallery. Taken from a leading New Zealand arts publication, and claiming to be a critique of the Gallery's new exhibitions policy, it viciously attacked Sybil Knight's professional credibility.

Todd Parker-Brown seemed unashamed. "I see you've read my piece."

"You didn't approve of Sybil's appointment, Mr. Parker-Brown?"

"None of us did," he replied with confident disdain. "Sybil was nothing more than an enthusiastic amateur. She was barely published."

"You wanted her job, Mr. Parker-Brown?" Amanda asked.

He gave a short thin laugh. "Hundreds of people wanted her job. I applied. I'm not denying it."

"I understand Sybil was your immediate superior."

He flushed, obviously niggled by Amanda's choice of words. "This is a creative environment rather than a workplace hierarchy as you know it, Inspector. We take an adult approach to dividing tasks. I develop my own exhibition and publication projects and discuss these with the Management Team."

Well excuse me, Amanda thought. "How would you describe your working relationship with Sybil?"

"There were issues, of course." He shrugged. "The Gallery is committed to a reconsideration of the dominant meanings of cultural forms. Sybil did not seem to have a full understanding of the artistic concerns, indeed the responsibilities, that accompany this process."

He cast a smugly assessing glance from Amanda to Austin Shaw, as though to satisfy himself that they had not understood a word he had said but would be impressed all the same.

Impassively, Shaw asked, "Where were you between two and four in the morning yesterday, Mr. Parker-Brown."

He stared as if he were the victim of a tasteless practical joke. "I was asleep in my bed. Seriously, you can't imagine I had anything to do with it ... I'm very sorry about what happened to her, of course ... I —"

"You and Sybil were heard arguing on the day she was murdered," Amanda broke in blandly. "What was that about?"

"It was purely a professional matter. Sybil had made some inappropriate alterations to a Gallery publication I'd written. I had to explain that I had my professional reputation to protect." Dismissively, he stood, a stark statement in black trousers, black polo-neck and a pewter medallion in an abstract design. "Now, if you've quite finished, I have a catalog to write."

Amanda remained in the hideously uncomfortable triangular chair the Gallery had provided for their makeshift interview room. "Do you deny saying 'I'll kill that bitch'?"

He seemed to have difficulty replying. "I ..."

"Sit down please, Mr. Parker-Brown," Shaw requested politely. "The Inspector has asked you a question."

"In the heat of the moment I may have said something like that." Parker-Brown resumed his seat, legs and arms crossed. "I really can't remember."

"When did you last see Sybil Knight?" Amanda asked.

"In the evening. Around seven."

"You were both working late?"

44

His murky eyes fastened on Amanda. "You people are so transparent," he sneered. "I can see what you're trying to do."

Shaw must have sensed Amanda's flare of annoyance. Smoothly, he picked up the questioning, "When did you leave the building Mr. Parker-Brown?"

With a gesture of mock-defeat, their subject sagged back in his chair. "Okay, I'll play the game. I left at seven-thirty."

"What did you do then?" Shaw continued pleasantly.

"I went to a bar . . . the Opera. I was meeting someone."

Shaw asked for a name and address. After much protestation, Parker-Brown provided it.

"Did you spend the night with this woman?" Amanda asked.

He shook his head. "I had other plans."

Struck out, huh? Amanda smiled slightly. "Did you return to the Gallery?"

"No. I went home."

"You live alone?"

"Yes."

"So no one can verify your whereabouts . . ." Amanda raised an eyebrow. "Pity."

Parker-Brown looked like prey the cat was feigning disinterest in.

Amanda thanked him for his help. "No doubt we'll see you again, Mr. Parker-Brown," she said pleasantly.

* * * * *

Leaving Austin Shaw to continue inquiries at the Gallery, Amanda drove along Oriental Parade.

The morning was sunless, the sea and the sky uniformly troubled. Thrown up by the overnight storm, great strands of leafy seaweed lined the Parade, litter entangled in its clammy foliage. There were broken umbrellas, bedraggled items of clothing, frayed roofing iron.

A water main had burst at the turnoff to Roseneath and the area swarmed with Council drainage workers in yellow plastic coats and matching hats. As she drove by, Amanda caught laughter, the strains of a Dolly Parton song playing on a truck radio, and felt suddenly at home.

Dr. Marlene Friedman operated her psychiatry practice from her home on the moneyed slopes of Roseneath. It was a ritzy address — everything very white — the pavements, the houses, the residents. This was the kind of neighborhood where you could take an evening stroll without ever tripping over broken bottles and stray dogs.

Dr. Friedman's house was an ultra-modern design perched on the cliff-side. With some difficulty, Amanda identified the front door, pressed the bell and fed her name into the intercom. A moment later the wall seemed to move. In the recess created, a woman stood.

Marlene Friedman was not at all as Amanda had imagined her. Instead of a colorless semi-formal suit and squarish glasses, she wore a shimmering silk brocade waistcoat over a butter yellow shirt and striped trousers. Her thick black hair was drawn tightly into a French plait emphasizing strong bone structure and spectacular earrings, each a stud from which several different jewels were suspended by long gold threads.

Amanda could not fathom her age. Forty? Her posture was effortlessly straight and she walked with the energy of a woman who exercised regularly. Following her through an entrance hall paneled with chrome and mosaic tiles, Amanda enjoyed her subtle perfume, an elegant oriental fragrance she did not recognize.

The area they entered was bright with refracted light, its ceiling extending to the level above. Floor-length windows formed a 180 degree arc capitalizing on a seascape that extended from tranquil Evans' Bay to the deep green open sea and around the tip of the Roseneath promontory to Wellington harbor. Rain distorted the view, slithering in rivulets down the windows.

"Coffee?" Dr. Friedman placed a promising-looking brew on an irregularly shaped glass table.

"Thank you. Black, no sugar." Amanda settled into an armchair wondering if this was where Dr. Friedman saw her patients. She fought off an immediate urge to apologize for wasting the psychiatrist's time. She said, "Sybil Knight was a patient of yours, I gather."

"A client and a friend," Dr. Friedman corrected pleasantly.

"How long have you known her?"

"I met Sybil four years ago."

"You began treating her then?"

Dr. Friedman sipped her coffee. "I first saw Sybil professionally a year ago." She did not expand.

Interpreting her reticence as that of any health professional concerned with client confidentiality,

Amanda said, "I understand Sybil spent Sunday night with you — the night before she died."

"That's right."

"Is it common for your clients to stay nights?"

Dr. Friedman lifted her well-defined eyebrows. "What are you asking me, Inspector Valentine? If we were having an affair?"

A little taken aback by her directness, Amanda said, "Were you?"

"Sybil was a client and a friend. There was nothing romantic between us." Her dark eyes overflowed. Taking a tissue from a box on her table, she sobbed calmly, blew her nose, and added, "Remarkable isn't it, this urge to feel responsible for the death of another person. I've gone over that night so many times. Was there something I might have done to alter the course of destiny? Could I have kept her here and stopped it happening?"

"Why did she visit on Sunday night?"

"She was feeling down. She had quarreled with her partner."

"What was that about?"

"We didn't discuss details."

Oh sure. Sybil Knight scuttles off to her therapist after a fight with her lover and they don't talk about it. "Dr. Friedman, do you know who killed Sybil?"

Marlene Friedman paled. "I have no idea."

"Did Sybil ever mention anyone she was afraid of or had some long standing grievance with?"

"Sybil had a great deal of anxiety around her relationships generally. I really can't be more specific than that."

"Can't?" Amanda met her eyes.

48

"Inspector, I'm willing to help you in any way I can."

We'll see, Amanda thought. "Sybil's case file." She tried her luck. "May I have it?"

"I was hoping you wouldn't ask." Marlene Friedman sounded genuinely regretful. "Those notes are strictly confidential."

"Sybil is dead," Amanda reminded her crisply.

"But other people are alive. I've agreed to answer your questions, but I cannot hand over a set of records which could prove hurtful. If the file contained anything relevant . . ."

"I don't think you're equipped to judge the relevance of its contents." Amanda was conscious of her own increasing irritation. "This is a criminal investigation. I could obtain a Court order."

Marlene Friedman was unmoved. "So get one. That file contains a record of one woman's attempt to resolve some very confusing family issues. Taken out of context, the material could hurt the people who loved Sybil best. I will not permit that to happen if I can help it."

Amanda backed off a little. "Okay. So tell me about Sybil, Dr. Friedman."

"Please call me Marlene." The psychiatrist relaxed into her chair, apparently more comfortable with this line of questioning. "Sybil came across as a very sophisticated person. It was a veneer perfected over many years to compensate for quite extraordinarily low self-esteem. She led a compartmentalized existence. In a way this made it easy for her to look good. No one ever saw her all of the time. I don't think many people knew her at all."

"And you?"

"It was no different for me." Marlene Friedman gave a small, wry grimace. "Except, perhaps, that I challenged her behavior. When Sybil first became my client, she presented herself as depressed . . . suicidal. At the time I felt she had issues around self-acceptance as a result of her lesbianism. She was very much in denial over her sexuality, even after several relationships with women. Gradually, with therapy, she became more secure in her identity."

"How would you describe her relationship with her family?"

"Very carefully." Marlene offered a professional smile. "It was no better or worse than anyone else's. The Knights are wealthy people. Sybil was brought up with traditional values and expectations. In some ways she failed to conform and in others she was a product of her environment."

Amanda called to mind Lady Knight's view of her daughter. "Would you describe her as naive?"

Marlene hesitated. "Thoughtless, perhaps. But not naive. I can see how she may have given that impression. Many wealthy young women do. They simply assume they can have what they want — the world is their department store."

"So it's possible Sybil may have acted insensitively toward others?" Recalling Kim Curtis's oblique references to relationship troubles, Amanda pondered again on the cause. Kim had seemed quite sure Sybil was not carrying on with her therapist and Marlene Friedman certainly didn't come across as anyone's "bit on the side." Had Sybil simply started taking her lover for granted? Or was Kim Curtis simply the insecure type?

"In some situations Sybil may have lacked empathy," Marlene observed. "She was working on her interpersonal skills."

"Sybil's partner mentioned a support group . . ."

"It's not a professional group." Marlene's tone hinted at disapproval. "I gather they met at a weekend seminar and decided to continue seeing each other regularly."

"Could you give me a contact name?"

Marlene hesitated. "Some of the people involved in groups like this are very vulnerable."

"I'll do my best not to stomp on anyone's sensibilities while I locate Sybil's murderer," Amanda said coolly.

With clear reluctance, the psychiatrist wrote on a small card and handed it over. "What do you enjoy about being a homicide detective, Inspector?"

It had to happen, Amanda thought. Marlene Friedman was bugged by her attitude and now she was going to analyze her. "It satisfies me," she responded unhelpfully. "How about you? Why psychiatry?"

Marlene looked thoughtful, her dark eyes roaming Amanda's face as though seeking something. "I love to solve mysteries. I suppose we have that in common. We both have to look beyond the obvious."

"Sometimes the obvious can be very hard to see," Amanda remarked.

"We focus so determinedly on shadows, we overlook substance?"

"Something like that." Amanda recalled several of the truly gruesome homicides she had investigated over the past twelve years. Relatives and friends of a killer so often missed the most blatant clues to his deeds. When you were looking for a monster, it was easy to miss the guy next door. Or in your own house.

CHAPTER SIX

Parked in Sybil Knight's driveway a little ahead of the time she had arranged with Kim Curtis, Amanda rummaged in her pockets. She located the slip of paper Marlene Friedman had given her and tapped the number into her cellular phone.

The contact for Sybil's support group was a man called Simon Elliot. His phone was answered breathily by a woman who said, "Welcome to Elliot Media. How may we add value to your life or business?"

For a split second Amanda contemplated her private wish-list — a luxury apartment, the girlfriend of her dreams, or if that wasn't possible, Cybill Shepherd. "Could I speak with Simon Elliot," she said. "This is Detective Inspector Amanda Valentine, Wellington CIB."

There was a sharp intake of breath. "Certainly, ma'am. Would you hold please."

Amanda tapped her fingers to the strains of some baroque music that would never reach a climax. A moment later she was told Simon would take her call.

"Amanda?" He sounded as if he knew her from way back. "Simon Elliot. What can I do for you?"

"I'm investigating Sybil Knight's death, Mr. Elliot. I was given your name as a contact for a support group Sybil attended. Would you mind answering a few questions about the group?"

"Not at all," Simon assured her. "I want to say right now that I honor your work, Amanda. We could get together tomorrow but hey, the group's meeting tonight. Perhaps you could come along?" Of course he would have to get the group's permission at the beginning of the session, he added, but given the circumstances . . .

Amanda thanked him sincerely and took down the address he gave.

"Sybil was a beautiful human being," he told her. "We connected very deeply."

Detective Marty Nikora was waiting on Sybil's doorstep. A hulking youngster, he was, according to a rapturous Joe Moller, destined to save the CIB Homicide rugby team from certain defeat at the hands of Uniform Branch. In the meantime Joe had confined him to desk duties, well out of harm's way. Feeling sorry for the kid and figuring she could use a detective who was champing at the bit, Amanda had assigned him to the Lynx case that morning.

Despite his obvious enthusiasm, Amanda found herself missing Janine Harrison's presence. Determined to provide Harrison with a cooling off period whether she liked it or not, Amanda had ordered the unhappy young woman to report to Joe Moller for duty on the Aro Valley investigation. At the morning briefing Harrison had refused to meet her eyes.

Kim Curtis let them in. She was in bad shape, still wearing pajamas, her mouth chewed raw and her eyes puffy from recent tears. Gesturing across the hallway, she said dully, "The papers you wanted are in the drawing room."

Suspending her coat on a hook inside the door, Amanda followed her across the hallway.

The scent of flowers lingered as it often did in the homes of the dead. Untidy stacks of paper littered the smooth walnut top of a large writing desk.

"It's all there," Kim said wanly. "These are to do with the Gallery, and these are letters to be answered." She lifted one bundle after another. "I don't know where to start."

Amanda found her mind wandering. The clothes would come next, she thought. There was something about your dead lover's clothing, the promise of her presence trapped in its fibers, the faint enduring fragrance of her. After Kelly was killed, it had been two months before Amanda could open her wardrobe. Folding away the material reminders of her lover's existence had been excruciating.

Amanda approached the desk. "It's okay, Kim," she said. "You don't have to do it alone. You've got friends . . ."

"I know." Hugging herself, Kim retreated into an armchair, wiping her face on her shirt-sleeve. "I'm sorry. I just can't seem to get a grip."

"Who says you have to?"

"I want to." Kim's sobs subsided into thin hiccups. "Someone killed Sybil and I don't want to be falling apart when I could be helping catch them." Her eyes appealed. "Do you have any idea who it was?"

"We have a lot of work to do, before I can say. It's very important that we trace Sybil's movements over the past week or so. We need to know everyone she saw, everywhere she went . . ."

"That's easy." Kim managed a weak smile. "It's all in her Filofax."

"You have that?"

Kim shook her head, faintly bewildered. "She always carries . . . carried it with her."

Amanda frowned. She could not recall any mention of a Filofax in Austin Shaw's meticulous inventory of the deceased's possessions. "Did Sybil keep a personal diary, Kim?"

"It's on the desk. She wrote in it every night before bed."

"This?" Amanda held up a small hardbound book. "Can you remember the last time you saw her do that?"

56

Kim hesitated. "I think it was the week before . . . it happened."

Fighting the urge to open the small red volume immediately, Amanda asked, "Is it okay for me to read this?"

"Go ahead."

Sybil had been murdered on Monday night, her body discovered on Tuesday. The last entry in her diary showed no date, but was headed Friday — possibly the Friday immediately prior to her death.

Today for the first time in weeks I feel comfortable with myself. It's as though I've just woken from a bad dream. I've been so scared but I'm sure everything will be all right now. Thank God for Marlene.

Amanda looked up. "So you and Sybil were having a rough patch," she proceeded cautiously. "And you quarreled on Sunday night. Was there a particular issue . . ."

Kim's shoulders shook. "No. I can't even remember how it started. It was just one of those stupid arguments. She never seemed to be there. She was always working late or seeing Marlene or going to her precious goddamn support group. I guess this sounds awful. Like I'm a real clinging vine. Well I'm not."

Giving her time to calm down, Amanda spent a few moments sorting Sybil's papers, cramming everything of possible interest into the file box she had brought with her.

"As we piece together Sybil's movements over the past week or so," she said, deliberately steering the discussion into more comfortable terrain, "it would help if you could write down anything you can remember about last week — phone calls, messages, letters, hours she was home, where she was staying if she was away any night..."

"Sure," Kim said huskily. "But I might forget some things."

"Just take your time. Think about your own movements each day. Then try and remember where Sybil was at the time."

"I'll do my best." Kim walked to the front door with Amanda and Detective Nikora. "I appreciate your kindness, Inspector."

Amanda gave her shoulders a quick hug. "I can't make any promises, you know."

Kim nodded. "I'll take my chances."

"When will we have the autopsy findings?" Amanda stalked into the inquiry center, shaking rain off her jacket.

Austin Shaw looked up from his PC, another of his faultless reports doubtless in progress. "I'm not sure. I left after Moira completed her preliminary examination. I believe they're still working, so I doubt we'll see the report until tomorrow afternoon."

"Call them," Amanda said. "Tell them I want that report on my desk in the morning or the Chief will get involved."

Shaw looked faintly taken aback. "I think they're aware the case has priority."

"Remind them." Dismissing him, Amanda cleared enough space on a desk for Sybil Knight's papers and diaries and began to reconstruct the movements of the victim in the hours, days, weeks prior to her death.

Sybil Knight appeared to have had a serious time management problem, one she compensated for by writing reminder notes to herself. Unfortunately, these were generally undated and were scribbled on yellow post-its which, Amanda assumed from the sticky little clusters, she periodically purged from her Filofax. Using the work schedule obtained from the City Gallery, Amanda sketched out Sybil's last two weeks, then started on her diary.

The entries were mostly short and undated but seemed chronological. They revealed a Sybil of rapid, often extreme, mood swings:

Today my body feels drained. My feelings are those of fear. I am upset to see Kim's anger. What part of myself is she mirroring?

And later, apparently on the same day, a complete about-face.

I love myself. I now have more emotional control of my life than ever before.

There was something peculiar about Sybil's perspective, Amanda thought, some odd detachment. For all that her diary appeared to be an intensely personal account of her feelings, it was almost as though a third party had made the observations. And there was virtually no information about the events that occurred in her life.

Amanda paused over a page Sybil had circled in red ink.

At last I am opening up to the joyful, sensual child within. I trust my aliveness and power. I am healing my life.

It was followed by a plethora of verbiage in a similar vein. Amanda searched vainly for a date. Abruptly the tone changed.

How could I have been so stupid? What is wrong with me? I am disgusting.

Pages of self-condemnation followed. Then, in an abrupt change of tone, Sybil's final entry, on the page marked Friday.

Today for the first time in weeks I feel comfortabble with myself. It's as though I've just woken from a bad dream. I've been so scared but I'm sure everything will be all right now. Thank God for Marlene.

Wondering what could account for such a change of attitude, she extracted Marlene Friedman's card from her file. When she got the doctor on the phone, Amanda said, "There's something else I need to ask you."

"Go ahead." Marlene sounded polite but cool.

"Apart from Sunday night, did you see Sybil last week?"

"Yes."

"When was that?"

Momentary silence. "We met on Wednesday afternoon."

"Not Friday?"

More silence. "Why do you ask?"

"I'm attempting to reconstruct Sybil's movements over the last days of her life," Amanda said briskly. "I thought she might have seen you on Friday."

"I'm sorry, I can't help you," Marlene Friedman replied.

Liar. Amanda noted the tiny voice of her subconscious. Deciding she would do a little more homework before she pursued that line of questioning, she said, "On Sunday night when Sybil stayed with you, do you remember what she had with her?"

"What do you mean?"

"Did she have some kind of overnight case? A handbag? Her Filofax?"

"Just her handbag."

"Normally she packed a case?"

"Oh yes. Sybil was very particular about that type of thing. But as I said, she wasn't planning to stay."

"Do you know what made her change her mind?"

"I must admit I was surprised," Marlene said. "She seemed to have resolved her fight with Kim. She was leaving, then she stopped and asked if she could stay the night."

"Could you tell me exactly what happened, Marlene?"

"I opened the door and we stood there for a minute or two talking." She paused. "We said good-bye, she started walking away, then suddenly she turned around and came back up the steps . . ."

"She was walking to her car?"

"Yes. That's another thing. When Sybil stayed she always brought the car into the garage. This time she'd parked at the curb."

"So she came up the stairs and asked if she could stay the night. How did she seem? What did you notice about her?"

"I can't believe I didn't think about this until now." Marlene sounded frustrated. "There was something. She looked . . . nervous."

"Just nervous?"

When Marlene spoke again her voice wavered.

"Frightened. I thought she seemed frightened. Oh my . . ."

"Marlene," Amanda cut across the trace of panic. "I want you to think very carefully. You were watching her leave. Did you notice anything unusual . . . cars, people?"

She heard Marlene catch her breath. "No . . . I can't see the road from my house anyway. Oh damn."

"It's okay. Don't force it. But if you think of anything else, no matter how insignificant it might seem, give me a call."

"Inspector . . . Amanda?"

"Yes, Marlene."

There was a long silence. "Forget it. Just a moment of helplessness. Perhaps it's something you bring out in a woman."

Amanda blinked.

"You can take that as a compliment," Marlene said softly.

Replacing the phone, Amanda repeated the phrase beneath her breath, trying to assess the subtext. There was none, she told herself. Just a touch of egomania on her own part. She checked her watch. Sybil's support group was meeting in less than an hour.

Glancing in Austin Shaw's direction, she said. "Ever done group therapy, Shaw?"

The man was ridiculously handsome, she reflected; tall, dark haired, impeccable taste in clothes. She was aware that most of her team could not fathom his choice of career, imagining television soap opera as the logical showcase for his talents. But Austin Shaw was the textbook homicide detective: relentless, obsessed with detail, a brilliant problem solver, a man who seemed to have no personal life.

Amanda knew only the barest details about him — that his mother was a brilliant violinist and that his father, a doctor, had left the family when Austin was very young. While his mother had trained in Paris and London, Austin had been reared by his maternal grandparents. Now deceased, they had, according to police rumor, left Austin and his mother a large amount of money.

Speculation about Austin Shaw's sexuality was also rife. Not surprising, Amanda thought. The man was handsome, unmarried, fastidious in his personal grooming and bought season tickets to the opera. Where some cops decorated their wall partitions with rugby calendars, Shaw had chosen a photo essay of dark and uncertain subject.

"Group therapy?" He turned warily toward Amanda. "Where is this leading, Inspector?"

Amanda smiled. "Get your coat. This could be the first day of the rest of your life."

CHAPTER SEVEN

The support group met at the community center in Mt. Victoria. Everyone was jogging in place when Amanda and Austin Shaw arrived.

A gangly man waved from the front of the room. "Hey there. Take off your shoes and come on over."

"Is he out of his mind?" Shaw glanced protectively at his Italian brogues.

"Find your pulse." Simon Elliot's commands reverberated off the timber walls. "Connect with your energy. Draw it up. Now slower, slower . . . Lie down. Breathe . . ."

Psychoaerobics, Amanda reflected. Get fit while you process.

The group lay around on mats for a few minutes, then adjourned to a semi-circle of chairs.

"Why are they here?" a very thin woman asked.

Simon smiled placidly. "That was a very direct question, Kathy. Thank you."

The thin woman flushed slightly.

Amanda formally introduced herself and Shaw and offered identification. The group nodded over this like inexperienced diners approving a bottle of wine.

"Amanda and Austin wish to ask us some questions about Sybil," Simon explained. "Is everyone comfortable with that?"

Four people carefully observed Amanda. A voluptuous woman with henna red dreadlocks said, "Hi, I'm Bernadette." She held back a sob. "Sybil meant a lot to me."

"Let it go, Bernie." Simon took her hand. "We're here for you."

As Bernadette applied a paper towel to her face, her companions introduced themselves. Although no one objected to the police presence, the atmosphere seemed thick with the unspoken.

Before Amanda could frame her first question, dreadlocked Bernadette observed, "Remember the first time Sybil came to the Group . . ."

"I was angry with her," undernourished Kathy said. "She looked so beautiful. She always wore the most fabulous clothes."

"Her hair was naturally that color," Bernadette marveled.

"How did you meet?" Amanda asked.

Everyone linked hands. Choked with emotion, Bernadette said, "We did the ACW training together."

"ACW?" Austin Shaw looked up from his note-taking, pen poised.

"Access the Child Within," Simon translated. "Remember the Trust Game . . ." He stared lovingly around the group. "It blew me away."

"Would you mind sharing that," Amanda invited.

Simon glanced first at Bernadette, then at a slim sandy-haired man in an Armani business suit. "Okay, guys?"

The sandy-haired man shrugged bleakly. He had introduced himself earlier as David Jordan and confessed to being in banking.

"I'm not sure . . ." Bernadette sounded apologetic. "I feel kind of exposed right now."

Amanda recalled several references to the lessons of "The Game" in Sybil's diary. "I gather this Game was important to Sybil."

"It changed her life," Simon said. "Have you played, Amanda?"

"No."

The group exchanged looks, their faces filled with the pitying condescension Amanda usually associated with Jehovah's Witnesses.

Kathy took a break from worrying a spot on her neck to offer a word of comfort. "I couldn't handle it either."

"When was this workshop?" Amanda asked.

"It feels like another lifetime, so much has

happened." Wonder entered Simon's tone. "But I guess it's only six months, eh, Bernie?"

"I miss her," said Bernadette. "How could anyone do that to her?"

Sandy-haired David plucked at his gold cufflinks with a delicately boned hand. "We live in a sick world, Bernadette. Human life counts for nothing."

"Karmically speaking, the murderer is as much a victim as Sybil," Simon offered.

"Only not as dead," Amanda commented dryly.

"Do you think you'll catch the guy?" Kathy gazed with hungry awe at Austin Shaw, who seemed benignly unaware of her attention. "What do you suppose she was doing in that place anyway?" she added. "I think it's weird."

"We can't say at this stage. But we have a lot of people to talk to —" Amanda cast a small lure. "People who saw her there that night." She met Bernadette's eyes, noting with interest a flicker of agitation.

David, the pretty banker, also seemed ill at ease. Amanda wasn't sure whether to put this down to talk of a dead woman, or the shame commonly engendered in respectable people by their own fear of involvement.

"When was the last time you saw Sybil?" Amanda asked the group.

"She missed last Wednesday," Simon said, adding, with a quick glance at David, "Didn't you have lunch with her some time recently?"

This interested Shaw, who observed, "Tuesday, wasn't it?"

David seemed astonished. "How ..."

"Remarkable what people remember," Austin informed the group. "A waiter served Sybil and a gentleman matching Mr. Jordan's description last week."

"You were a personal friend of Sybil's?" Amanda asked the banker.

His clear blue eyes lifted to meet hers. "That's right." He seemed perilously close to tears, yet Amanda was certain she caught a hint of challenge in his tone.

"I'm surprised her partner didn't mention you," she said.

David shrugged, color climbing his high-boned cheeks. "Sybil led her own life."

"Kim didn't support Sybil," Bernadette inserted. "She was incredibly possessive."

Noting the hint of protectiveness, Amanda continued questioning David. "Did you often meet Sybil privately?"

"Sometimes." David Jordan's expression combined defensiveness with maligned innocence.

Nothing unusual, Amanda knew. Most people questioned over their connection to a murder victim seemed to feel they had to prove themselves innocent. Detectives knowingly played on this, sometimes implying suspicion and disbelief until a guilty conscience revealed itself.

Amanda glanced assessingly about the group. "Anyone else have contact with Sybil outside of your meetings?" No one came forward. "We believe Sybil knew her killer," she went on. "And that means some of her acquaintances know this person too."

There was a general intake of breath. David

surreptitiously wiped his hands on the underside of his seat.

"If any of you have information which may be relevant, please call the Station."

Austin Shaw handed out cards while Amanda buttoned her coat. She could almost hear the sighs of relief as they left the room.

"Inspired detective work." Amanda waited till they were in the car to address Shaw. "I read that damned report before we left and I didn't make the connection."

"You didn't interview the waiter," Shaw commented. "He remembered David Jordan very well — the guy sent his meal back."

"Check him out. There's something about him . . ." Amanda felt niggled. She gave the feeling some room. "He reminds me of Sybil's brother."

"Because they're both blond?" Austin Shaw's tone suggested he thought Amanda should probably call it a night. "White, male, privileged . . ."

Amanda rolled her eyes. "Give me a break."

The inquiry center was quiet, the Desk Sergeant and brawny Detective Nikora present. They were watching television.

"You're just in time, ma'am," Nikora said cheerfully. *The Late News.*"

"I can hardly wait," Amanda muttered.

So far the media had circled like restless dogs, contenting themselves with a few scraps in the apparent certainty of a feast to come. They had run the story, of course. But their tone had been respectful and disinterested, Sybil's murder described as *The tragic death in suspicious circumstances of Wellington City Gallery's Principal Curator.*

It couldn't continue, Amanda thought. She had bought a day's grace from television and the tabloids, perhaps two from the more respectable print media. Mentioning the Knight family's enthusiasm for costly litigation had probably helped. The Chief was happy. All they needed now was a nice tidy arrest, preferably of an escaped high-security mental patient, a quick trial and a maximum sentence. The case would be forgotten in a week.

Munching on potato crisps, Nikora was laughing at footage of Austin Shaw in front of the Station. "Jeez, you look like that guy they interviewed on *Entertainment Tonight*. The new James Bond. What's his name? ... That movie star ... better looking than Tom Cruise."

"Pierce Brosnan?" Amanda suggested.

"Yeah, that's him. I reckon you should think about it, sir," Nikora advised. "All that money, women throwing their knickers at you ..."

"I'll bear that in mind." Shaw's tone was damp. Casting a faintly apologetic look at Amanda, he remarked, "The coverage seems quite restrained."

"I imagine the station executives spent the day taking legal advice," Amanda said cynically. "Finding out how far they can go before Sir George Knight sets his lawyers onto them."

She watched the images on the small screen. Sybil's body being removed from the Lynx, Casey Randall declining to comment, the City Gallery Director holding back tears.

Austin Shaw moved to his desk as the news item concluded. "That Filofax you asked about . . . we definitely don't have it. Several people at the Gallery saw her with it on Monday. I searched her office — no luck."

Amanda mentally recapped on their interviews with Gallery staff. Most people seemed to be in a state of shocked incomprehension, and were anxious to help. Todd Parker-Brown was the exception. "What did you think of Parker-Brown?" Amanda asked Shaw.

"I think it's fair to say we can't rule him out just yet." Shaw was never premature in his conclusions. "I have something that will interest you." He handed Amanda several large sheets of computer paper, explaining, "This is the security printout for Monday night. It shows everyone who entered and exited the Gallery building using their MIL security keys. I've marked Sybil Knight's codes."

Amanda gazed at the small red arrows. Sybil had entered the building at 02:08am, departing ten minutes later at 02:18am. An hour later she was back again, at 03:20am, exiting at 03:25am. It didn't make any sense. "If time of death was approximately three a.m., either Moira's wrong or . . ." A small rush of adrenaline made her catch her breath. "Someone used Sybil's MIL key."

"Well, it wasn't among her possessions." Shaw thumbed the inventory, his expression intent.

Amanda met his eyes. "I guess it wouldn't be if the killer has it." Her thoughts raced. "They have security cameras at the Gallery, don't they?"

"Only in the viewing rooms," Shaw replied. "All the internal doors are controlled electronically. You have to use a MIL key to get in or out."

"Did the guards see anything?"

He shook his head. "They patrolled at two thirty and three thirty."

So they had missed the second visitor by minutes. Perhaps it was Sybil, Amanda thought. It was notoriously difficult to estimate the time of death. Pathologist Moira had suggested 03:00am. She could be wrong.

"We need that damned autopsy report," Amanda grumbled.

"We'll have it at ten in the morning," Shaw advised in a placatory tone.

Amanda read the printout again. "Check all the other codes. I want the names of every person who went in or out of the Gallery that day. Let's see if Parker-Brown was telling us the truth about his departure time."

Sybil had left the Gallery at 02:18. Amanda's thoughts flicked to Casey Randall. What time had she left the Lynx?

Shaw must have asked himself the same question. Scanning his computer files, he said, "According to Casey Randall's statement, she left the Lynx at about twenty past two."

"Which makes her . . ." Even as she considered the possibility, Amanda was conscious of an urge to deny it.

"A prime suspect?" Shaw completed quietly.

CHAPTER EIGHT

The Lynx was packed. Blinking into the bluish haze of the dance floor, Amanda elbowed her way through a sea of sweating female bodies to the bar. Someone wearing an executioner's mask promptly arrived alongside and asked if she was looking for some action.

Pleading vanilla, Amanda signaled the hunky blond behind the bar, and asked for Casey Randall.

This character dismissed her with a glance. "She's busy."

My, all that and charm too. Amanda eyed the

barperson's earrings, caught a glimpse of breast beneath her leather jerkin, and produced a becoming smile. "Do yourself a favor." She extended her identification. "Tell your boss I'm here."

The barwoman was the essence of cool. Picking up the phone, she muttered something and gestured in the direction of the staircase. "Go on up."

Casey Randall was waiting at the top of the stairs, her daytime conservatism cast off in favor of nightclub gear. Dark hair slicked back flat and shiny, she wore tight zippered black leather shorts, ankle boots and a studded bustier. The woman looked like she brunched on nubile schoolgirls.

"Well, this is an unexpected pleasure." She looked Amanda over. "I suppose it's redundant to ask what brings you here. You don't seem the kind of girl to party her nights away."

"Could we talk somewhere?" Amanda adopted her most no-nonsense manner.

"Sure. We have a discreet little parlor specially for wilting violets who can't be seen at queer venues."

Refusing to respond to this obvious baiting, Amanda said coolly, "I'm here on duty, Casey. It doesn't matter where I'm seen."

"If you say so, Inspector." Casey descended the stairs, Amanda behind her, and headed for the bar, where she seemed to be giving instructions to her graceless henchwoman.

Cooling her heels at the edge of the dance floor, Amanda let her gaze travel the room. The music was loud and repetitive, its thudding beat resounding against the walls of her chest.

The Lynx attracted a mixed clientele. Nice young things clutched their drinks and eyeballed the flesh-filled room with the terrified fascination of car crash witnesses, out-of-towners plunged periodically into the fray to attempt a two-step, locals cruised purposefully.

"Dance?" inquired a voice close to her ear.

Turning, Amanda found her body aligned with Casey Randall's. Their eyes locked. Amanda looked down first. A big mistake. Casey's smooth, creamy breasts seemed too full for their leather cups and deep in her cleavage was a small round tattoo. Amanda stared hard. It was an elaborate spiral design, bands of color weaving a rainbow pattern.

"Do you like my snake?" Casey leaned forward, her breath damply brushing Amanda's cheek. "You'll have to get close if you want to talk. We could dance now and do business later."

Amanda was sharply conscious of the heat, the pull of the music, the sexual energy of the crowd. Casey smiled and took a few paces back. Then they were dancing.

At first Amanda felt gauche. In her sensible grey flannel pants and black woolen jacket, she wasn't dressed for this. She was only grateful she had left her .357 in the car.

Although the police were not armed in New Zealand, Amanda had never quite adjusted to the idea of being on duty without her gun. Normally, using a liberal interpretation of police regulations, she could justify carrying her Smith & Wesson. Her rank helped. Tonight, however, she had felt unexpectedly ambivalent about taking a weapon into Casey Randall's club. Certainly the idea that her life might be in immediate danger at a lesbian venue in little New Zealand seemed far-fetched. But it was more than that. To Amanda's surprise and no little dismay, she was conscious of an odd yearning to fit in.

Ironic, really. As if a cop would ever find easy acceptance in the lesbian community. It was almost as likely as the police force welcoming lesbians to the ranks. She should have worn her damned gun, Amanda thought. She couldn't feel any more displaced, could she?

Casey Randall moved with controlled precision. Eyes closed, head tilted back, she seemed lost in the music. Amanda permitted herself a long hard look and concluded that the woman was overwhelmingly sexy.

Echoing some of Casey's moves, she wondered what was behind her overt flirting. Did she have something to prove or something to hide? The beat slowed. Casey locked her hands behind Amanda's hips and pulled her close, guiding her with her thighs. She was slightly shorter than Amanda, her body firm and strong. She smelled of leather, cigarettes and some faded scent.

Amanda slid her hands to the small of Casey's back and caught a flinty look from the barwoman. What was that about? she wondered. Was she jealous? Protective? Just plain aggro?

In her ear, Casey murmured, "Let's get out of here."

"It's a bit late for the cafes, but my place is near by." Casey threw Amanda a challenging sideways glance.

"Fine." Perfect in fact, Amanda told herself. A chance to check out the home of a suspect.

Taking her own car, she drove to the Majoribanks Street address Casey had given and found a parking place a few doors along. As she watched Casey pull into her garage, she donned her shoulder holster and checked that her gun was loaded. It was good to be back in familiar territory, she told herself — entering the residence of a possible suspect, taking no chances. Vigilant. Prepared. Appropriately paranoid.

Casey Randall's small duplex didn't feel much like the home of someone who would cold-bloodedly kill her best friend, but Amanda reminded herself that assumptions were the detective's quicksand. Casey flicked a switch and a series of spotlights lit up a narrow panelled hallway crowded with bookcases and potted plants. This led to a pristine kitchen.

"Thank God," Casey sighed. "Mrs. Jorgensen made it after all." Catching Amanda's eye, she added irreverently, "Good help is hard to find."

Amanda loitered in the doorway, hands tucked loosely into her pockets. She was very conscious of the shoulder holster strapped beneath her left arm — the unwieldy reminder that she was here on police business.

"What's your drug — caffeine or alcohol?" Casey opened a cupboard.

"I'd kill for a coffee."

"A crime of passion — I can relate to that." Casey heaped beans into the grinder. "Let me guess. Espresso, no cream, dash of sugar."

"Well, I'm impressed. I suppose you've got my zodiac sign figured, too."

"Child's play. You're a Leo." Casey grinned at Amanda's frowning assent.

The grinder revved into life and Amanda nearly fainted from pleasure. Fresh coffee — how long had it been?

With a small flourish, Casey switched the machine off and started the coffee brewing. "So, tell me, Inspector, are you one of the family or has my gaydar malfunctioned?"

For a moment Amanda hesitated, a little off-balance. Very few people had ever asked her directly about her sexuality. "I don't discuss my private life on the job," she responded.

Casey gave a knowing smile. "I'll read that as a yes."

They moved to a small adjoining conservatory where they sat in softly cushioned cane armchairs and sipped their coffee.

"Does it pay well — being a detective?" Casey inquired.

"I imagine the nightclub business is much more lucrative. Isn't that why you're in it?"

This earned a small ironic smile. "That's part of it. I think it's important to get a return on any investment."

Amanda sipped her coffee and released a slow satisfied sigh. "This is great."

"But now you want to talk shop?" Casey removed a cigarette from the packet on the small table beside her chair. "And here I was, all set to flirt with you."

Amanda let that one go. Finding a formal tone, she said, "I'm looking for something that belonged to Sybil — a Filofax."

"Her Filofax? Don't you people have it with her stuff?"

"Could you describe it?"

"The expensive type. Blue kid with her initials in gold on the spine."

"Do you know if Sybil had it with her on Monday night?"

"She would have," Casey said. "Some people have a memory, Sybil had a Filofax."

"Then it must be at the Lynx."

"Impossible," Casey was emphatic. "Except for what you people have sealed off, I had the place cleaned from top to bottom today. We would have found it."

"Are you quite sure Sybil had it with her the night she was killed?"

Casey's mouth thinned. "Do I strike you as a fool or merely a compulsive liar?"

"Did you actually see it?" Amanda persevered.

Casey drew heavily on her cigarette, brow knitted. Eventually a slight flush crawled into her cheeks. "I owe you an apology," she said. "Sybil wasn't carrying anything when she came in. She just had on her overcoat and her work clothes."

"Tell me about that night again," Amanda said quietly. "Picture it in your mind exactly as you saw it. Do you mind if I tape this?"

"Help yourself. But I'll deny everything when I'm arrested." She couldn't quite summon up a laugh at her own joke. "Sybil arrived around midnight. She'd been working late."

"Why did she park out back? The Gallery is virtually next door."

"Safety I guess. It's better to use a car late at night, even if it is only for a few yards."

"So, what did she do for the two hours she was here?"

"She had a few drinks. Danced . . ."

"With whom?"

Casey exhaled slowly. "With me."

"Anyone else?"

"No one important."

"Names?"

"I'm sorry." Casey was stubbornly unhelpful. "I don't remember."

"Please try," Amanda said. "Your friend is dead."

Casey tilted her head back, eyes closing briefly. "Look, I run a lesbian club. The police haven't done much to earn our confidence." Her voice thickened. "I could hand you a list of patrons and be out of business tomorrow. I'd do it if I thought you'd find the killer's name there. But you won't."

"What makes you so certain?"

Casey looked uneasy, self-doubt squeezing her brow. "I don't know quite how to say this . . . There was something going on for Sybil. Something had rattled her cage. I wondered about her and Kim."

"What did you wonder?"

"They seemed unhappy."

"Were you and Sybil lovers?"

Casey examined her cigarette. "Next question."

"Did you want to be her lover?"

"That's none of your business. Now, can we change the subject?"

Amanda gave a small obliging shrug. "Let's go back to Sybil's dancing partners. I'd like their names."

"Persistent, aren't you?" Casey's tone was sarcastic. "I like that in a woman."

Amanda wasn't biting. "Is there some reason you won't tell me who these women were?" She played the plodding investigator. "Are you trying to protect someone?"

Casey rolled her eyes. "Only Bernadette Lee, who would have been Sybil's sexual slave. Except that Sybil had standards."

"Bernadette . . ." The woman who had denied any contact with Sybil outside the support group. "Henna dreadlocks by any chance?"

"Clearly, you've met." Casey looked amused.

"Tell me about her and Sybil."

Casey gave a what's-to-say shrug. "There was nothing happening there. Bernie's a twelve-stepper with a chip on her shoulder. She and Sybil were brainwashed at the same self-awareness seminar last year. Syb was right into that three letter new age stuff — EST, LRT, ELI, NLP." Casey grimaced. "Now, I guess you're going to tell me you have a Lazarus calendar right by your bed."

Amanda cast her mind to the literature gathering dust on her bedside table. *Gun World,* the *Advocate,* the latest Alison Bechdel cartoons. "I don't get a whole lot of time for reading."

"How about a social life — do you have time for that?"

"Occasionally." Amanda gave a half-smile. "Do you have Bernadette Lee's address?"

Casey crossed the room to a computer work station and flicked through a card file. She wrote something on a sheet of paper and handed it to Amanda, adding, "I shouldn't be doing this, but I guess you'll only look in the electoral rolls if I don't tell you."

Amanda folded the note and tucked it into her breast pocket. "Was there anyone else dancing with Sybil?"

"No one I knew. A couple of lipstick girls. Sybil always fancied the pretty ones."

"You told me yesterday Sybil came to the Lynx often." Amanda could almost hear the Knight family's denials. "Did she ever use an upstairs room?"

"Are you asking me if Sybil had sex with casual partners?" Casey sounded faintly incredulous, as though waiting for Amanda to realize she had asked a deeply tasteless question about a dead woman.

"Did she?" Amanda asked.

Casey stubbed out her cigarette. "At one time."

"How did you feel about that?" And how did Kim Curtis feel, if she knew?

"It was Sybil's business how she chose to live." Casey's nonchalance seemed forced. "She was working through a few issues."

"Did she go upstairs with anyone on Monday night?"

"No. I've already told you —"

"Any idea how her partner felt about all this?"

"Kim was the perfect wife," Casey replied cynically. "She knew exactly how much slack to cut Sybil — just enough so she would feel insecure and run on back —" She fell silent, as if annoyed at herself.

Guessing Casey had revealed more than she intended, Amanda asked, "Were you in love with Sybil?"

Casey stared. "Ah, the jealous other woman theory." Shaking her head, she commented dryly, "It's hardly my scene Inspector. I'm not the obsessive type."

"You haven't answered the question."

"Of course I loved Sybil," Casey said after a drawn out silence. "For a time that translated as lust, but —" She shrugged. "Sybil needed a friend."

"How long did you know her?"

"Nine years. We met on a plane. Funny, huh?" Blinking away tears, she concentrated on her coffee.

Ignoring an impulse to comfort her, Amanda instead steered the conversation to Monday night. "You said Sybil left the Lynx at two in the morning on the night she died. Can you tell me about that."

"Again?" Casey cleared her throat. She seemed to relax suddenly, the digression to familiar questions apparently welcome. "The place was empty. I let the staff go. Sybil helped me lock up. I had to finish a bit of paperwork upstairs, so I let her out."

"Out where?"

"The front entrance."

"Why not the back? That was where her car was."

"She said she had left something at the Gallery." Casey's voice grew husky.

"When exactly did she walk out the door?"

"I'd say five past two."

"Was her car out back when you left?"

Casey nodded. "I figured she was still up in her office."

Amanda performed the calculations in her head. It took a couple of minutes to walk from the back entrance of the Gallery to the Lynx. The security records showed Sybil exiting at 02:18. How could Casey have missed her?

"So at two-twenty you got into your car and drove away. What did you see?"

Casey closed her eyes. "Nothing. No traffic. No pedestrians. I looked left and right. There were a few cars parked on the opposite curb."

"Their makes?"

Casey hesitated, her eyes still closed. "Modern. A couple of family sedans, a small van, a motorbike, and some kind of sports car."

"Anyone inside?"

"Not that I could see. It was very dark."

"You didn't hear anything?" Amanda felt conscious of her departure from procedure in questioning Casey Randall without a second officer present. If Casey made an admission now, it would be worthless as evidence.

"Everything was quiet," Casey said. Sliding her hands into her hair, she released a fractured sigh. "God, I wish I could turn the clock back. I should have waited for her. I should have gone to the Gallery with her. I nearly did."

It was a convincing show of self-blame. Caught between schooled cynicism and a continuing urge to wrap her arm around Casey's shoulders, Amanda stood. "If you think of anything else . . ."

"I have your card," Casey completed. She watched Amanda put on her jacket. "Had enough of my company already?"

Amanda's mouth dried. She allowed her eyes to trace a path from Casey's full kissable mouth to the tattooed snake nestling between her breasts.

Something went thud in the pit of her stomach. Casey Randall was very tempting, gift-wrapped in black kid. "I'm not here for fun," she said.

Casey met her eyes, sexual interest unmistakable. "And if you were?"

Amanda toyed with the key ring in her pocket. "I'd be looking for another job."

"Pity," Casey said candidly. "You don't know what you're missing."

Amanda met her eyes. "That's probably a good thing."

She took the coastal route home, her windows wound down to admit the steady pulse of the ocean. The sky was black, the moon appearing fitfully through dense cloud cover. On the surrounding hillsides, a few lights gleamed through the mist.

Amanda turned on her radio and got late night talkback — old people whose pasts loomed larger than the present. She twisted the dial.

"Are you lonesome tonight . . ." Elvis crooned.

Resigning herself, Amanda sang along.

CHAPTER NINE

Every city has an area described in tourist literature as a colorful neighborhood. In Wellington, it was the Aro Valley.

In the Valley, students, gays, aging hippies, poor people, immigrants, criminals, liberals and trendies, and their dogs, all rubbed elbows at Patel's grocery store on Aro Street. Valley residents took an interest in their community, and forced the local authorities to do the same by means of delegations, protests, press releases, and any other brand of negative publicity that could embarrass officials. Residents were unafraid of being labeled pinkos, queers, solo-mums, drug mafia, hippies, welfare bludgers, or trouble-makers — identities they cheerfully claimed. Only two epithets terrified them deeply — racist and yuppie.

Naturally, the doorknock had yielded an immediate response. The Aro Valley Residents' Association telephoned to lay a formal complaint of police harassment. The Sergeant helpfully passed the call on to Amanda.

A man identifying himself as Gilbert Friend, a spokesperson for the Association, demanded an official explanation of police conduct.

"My officers are investigating the disappearance of several children," Amanda responded politely. "They are carrying out routine inquiries in your area."

"Are you knocking on doors in Kelburn, too?" Friend demanded. "Of course you're not! You're only interested in hassling people who can't fight back."

Amanda waited in silence.

"Are you there?" said Mr. Friend.

"Yes."

"Well, we'd like to know how long this is going to take."

"Our inquiries will be completed as soon as possible."

"That doesn't tell me a thing."

"Perhaps I can put it more clearly," Amanda said coldly. "If my time, or that of my detectives, is wasted or we find ourselves obstructed in any way, our inquiries could go on indefinitely."

"Is that some kind of threat?"

"A promise, Mr. Friend."

As soon as he'd hung up, Amanda called Janine

Harrison. "What's going on down there? I've just had the Residents' Association on the phone bleating about police harassment."

"Harassment." Harrison seemed to choke. "We're falling over backwards to ignore their damned dope plants."

"What have you got so far?"

"You name it," Harrison groaned. "A confession from some guy who reckons aliens made him steal the kids for experiments on spaceships. A few unreported B&Es. Located two stolen vehicles. Vice is down here begging us to cut them in. We're going into the school this morning to take a few more statements."

"Hold till I get there will you, Harrison?"

There was an affronted silence. "The situation is in hand, ma'am. We've got the Maori Warden, a signer from the Deaf Association, Age Concern, the animal ambulance. We've laid on a caravan for the Community Law office. We're giving away free Cokes like this is the desert or something . . ."

Community relations. It was a topic at Police College, but nothing could prepare an officer for the Aro Valley.

"How about the media?" Amanda inquired.

"Pretty quiet. A couple of guys from the *Post* and the radio. No TV so far."

"Fine," Amanda said. "I'll be there in ten minutes."

There was a loud abrupt click. Harrison, Amanda surmised, had just managed to refrain from slamming the phone in her ear.

* * * * *

Leaving Austin Shaw to oversee the questioning of various individuals who were in the Civic Square vicinity on Monday night, Amanda drove the one-way route down Victoria Street to the Aro Valley.

Operation Truant was based in a Police Bus parked in the leafy turnaround where Aro Street met Holloway Road. Not only was the latter home to some of the last genuine communists, tramps and hippies in Wellington, but also to the largest dogs. These were, a tabloid had recently claimed, a mutant breed that had come about as a result of puppies being fed human breast milk. A cartoon depiction had been titled "Neanderthal Hound."

Holloway Road had its own Residents' Association. This splinter faction, convinced that the Valley was becoming overrun with opportunist trendies and their designer babies, had devised a plan for their street to secede from the city and declare itself an independent township.

Although the Holloway Road clan had never welcomed a police presence, they seemed mollified that it was bothering the rest of the Valley even more. In a rare demonstration of solidarity with the authorities, they had delivered a sack of organically grown carrots and a promise that no one would graffiti the bus.

As Amanda examined the data that had been collected so far, Joe Moller turned up with an espresso from the cafe down the road. Handing this to her, and adjusting his suspenders, he remarked cheerfully, "Well, we've got them on the run."

"The satanists?"

"The Association." He devoured a low-cal oaty bar.

"Any evidence?" Amanda tried not to sound as

impatient as she felt. Joe Moller's preoccupation with the Aro Valley case bothered her. He had always been the kind of stubborn cop who got hold of a scent and couldn't rest until he had traced the source. But Amanda wondered about his judgment this time round.

Operation Truant was exactly the kind of fishing expedition the CIB avoided, a potential flytrap that would suck up valuable resources for no result. She could close it down, but she was conscious of a deep reluctance to tread on her one-time partner's toes. It was guilt, she supposed. Guilt that she had made DI and Joe hadn't.

"There's more kids involved," Joe said. "Harrison's been down at the school counting heads. The rolls don't check out."

"Maybe they don't keep their records up to date."

Joe shook his head. "We've traced the missing kids — birth certificates, Social Welfare reports . . ."

"What about the parents?"

"Biggest pack of bloody liars. They're all on welfare . . . every last one of them. Not a father in sight, of course — useless bastards have probably skipped the country to avoid paying child support . . ."

Amanda felt a sharp stab of alarm. Perhaps she had discounted Joe's concerns too hastily. "Some of them must be worried if their kids are missing."

"Oh, yeah. They're real jumpy now," Joe said with satisfaction. "Now they know we've got a witness. This old lady knows everything. Seen the lot."

Amanda was scared to ask.

"Lives opposite that paddock behind the fish and

chip shop." Joe consulted his notes. "That's where they conduct their rites. I've got Uniform Branch down there digging the place up."

Amanda cradled her head in her hands. "Joe, I have a bad feeling about this."

Conveniently, Bernadette Lee lived in a seedy Victorian house just off Aro Street. Amanda called in on her way to meet Harrison at the local school. A sign on the door declared the house to be AN ALCOHOL AND DRUG FREE ZONE.

Amanda's knock was answered by a group of women who, at the sight of her identification, declared they were not cooperating with the police. If she didn't leave immediately they would take down her name and identification number and lay a complaint of harassment.

Tapping her foot, Amanda asked for Bernadette Lee.

"She's not here," said a lank-haired woman with braces on her teeth.

"Just piss off," shouted someone from a room upstairs.

Amanda attempted patience. "I need to speak to Bernadette about a friend of hers who has been murdered. When do you expect her?"

Protracted discussion ensued.

"She'll be home soon. You'd better wait in the kitchen," the lank-haired spokeswoman dourly invited. Introducing herself as Jo, she led Amanda along a cluttered hallway to a kitchen that smelled of garlic and cat pee. On the wall above an ancient stove, a large cross-stitch sampler bore the legend *One Day At A Time.*

"You clean?" inquired her hostess.

Amanda committed herself to an apologetic disclaimer. "I don't have a substance problem."

"I was like you," Jo informed her. "In denial. I didn't have a problem either, no ma'am, not me."

"What happened?" Amanda braved.

Jo slid her hands into the pockets of her floral overalls. "It was after I broke up with my ex. I felt like shit. I was doing dope and pills. Then one day I'm at the markets and there's this bag lady in Civic Square and she waves out and calls my name. Turns out it's this old friend of mine — only she's not that old."

"Pretty bad, huh?"

"Totally wasted. Fuck, what a trip." She dangled a sachet of recycled rosehip in a stained cup and handed the results to Amanda. "Well, that was six months ago. Since then I've been to hell and back."

"How did you meet Bernadette?"

"On the program. Bernie's incredible. Three years clean and sober." Jo peered at Amanda's watch. "She should be home soon. She's on the dawn shift."

"Where does she work?"

"She's a hotline volunteer for Lesbians United for Sobriety and Health."

"What about paid employment?"

Jo squinted. "Who did you say you were?"

Amanda found a card in her breast pocket and handed it over.

Jo read it at length, then turned it over as

though expecting to find some secret message encoded on the blank side. "Is this about Sybil Knight?" she finally asked.

Amanda gave a noncommittal smile. "Did you know Sybil?"

"Not exactly." Jo glanced swiftly across her shoulder as a door banged. "That'll be Bernie now." Getting to her feet she called, "Hey Bernie, there's a cop here to see you." With a quick, cautious glance at Amanda, she added, "They treated Bernie like shit."

"Who did?"

"Sybil Knight and Casey Randall."

"Really?"

Jo sniffed. "If you ask me, that rich bitch got exactly what was coming to her."

"That's a terrible thing to say." Bernadette slammed her satchel on the table and glared at Jo who retreated from the room.

"Sometimes you can be so thick, Bernie," Jo said from the doorway. "She was just using you."

"Please ignore Jo," Bernadette told Amanda. "She's in recovery. More tea?"

Amanda quickly shook her head.

"Let's go to my room. It's kind of public here."

Gratefully leaving her cup, Amanda followed Bernadette up a creaking staircase into a room whose excessive hominess was in stark contrast to the rest of the house. Amanda took in the swagged curtains, the frilled bedding starchy pink and obviously freshly made up that morning. On the highly polished dressing table, cosmetics were arranged like a military parade — lipsticks assembled next to eye-shadow, mascara wands upright in an embossed container, compacts stacked in precise piles, face creams arranged by night and day.

Bernadette's clothes would be hanging color-coded in her wardrobe, Amanda guessed; her shoes paired on racks and polished after she had worn them. Clearly the woman was a closet suburbanite stranded in the ghetto of lesbian downward mobility.

"Nice room," she observed, taking the small velvet chair Bernadette indicated. "How long have you been here?"

"It's my house. My mother left it to me."

"And the other women?"

"Friends who need a hand. You know how it is."

Sure. Mugs were born every day. "I understand you were with Sybil the night she was murdered," Amanda said casually.

Bernadette went bright red. "I didn't want to lie, but the Lynx is not exactly the kind of place . . . I mean, you never know how people will react. Lots of women want it closed down and now that this has happened . . ." She reached for a box of tissues.

"Did you see Sybil at the club often?"

Bernadette shook her head. "She had to be careful, with that job and everything. I think her family gave her a hard time, too."

"Tell me about that."

"Something happened with her brother." Bernadette lowered her voice. "She wouldn't talk about it, but you could tell. You know what I mean?"

"Are you saying Sybil's brother molested her?"

"It would explain a lot."

94

"Go on," Amanda encouraged.

Bernadette screwed up her face and blew her nose a couple of times. "Sybil was one of those people you can't get close to. I wanted to help her but she wouldn't let me. She was getting worse and no one could see it."

"When did you notice this?"

"Over the last few months. We were never really close or anything, but I liked her a lot."

"Any idea what was going on?"

Bernadette's gaze traveled the room as if she were seeking reassurance that her surroundings were in perfect order. "I don't know. That night — at the Lynx — she said she wanted some air. She asked me to walk with her. All the time we were walking, she kept looking around like she was watching for something. I asked her if she was all right..." Bernadette took a tissue break. "You know what she said? She said 'I hope so.' "

"What time did you leave the club?"

Bernadette looked vague. "I don't wear a watch. I guess it might have been one in the morning."

"What was Sybil doing?"

"She was with Casey. They were dancing."

Maintaining her methodic monotone, Amanda asked, "Were Sybil and Casey involved, Bernadette?"

"Not any more," Bernadette said. "But they were when Sybil met Kim. That's why they broke up. Sybil started seeing Kim, and Casey told her to choose."

And she chose Kim, Amanda added silently.

Bernadette wiped mascara from beneath her eyes.

"The funeral's on the weekend, isn't it?" Folding her arms across her body in a gesture of self-comfort, she walked Amanda to the door, adding gravely, "I don't think I can face it. Who needs another excuse to drink?"

CHAPTER TEN

Complaining bitterly, Janine Harrison accompanied Amanda across Aro Park to the school. "I don't know what their problem is. We could have made sixteen arrests already and we haven't even searched houses. This place is a law unto itself."

The School Administrator was a patient-looking woman somewhere in her forties. Winter clothing seemed too heavy for her, Amanda thought, taking in her elaborate silver and moonstone jewelry. Her grey hair was long and bushy, held back with an Indian scarf with small bells suspended from tassels at each end. She smelled faintly of patchouli. With a smile that was both welcoming and bewildered, she introduced herself as Pax Rainbow and expressed dismay at the investigation. "Of course we are anxious to find these children, but I don't think the parents will be happy when they know you've been here."

Amanda glanced around the shabby prefabricated buildings. "Is that an assembly hall?"

"Yes, but —"

"This is a small school. Rather than disturb each classroom, perhaps if you could assemble all the children together . . ."

"You mean now?"

Amanda nodded. "I understand your concerns, Ms. Rainbow. Naturally if any child comes forward with information, we will contact the parents immediately. We cannot interview a child without a parent or lawyer in attendance."

This seemed to mollify Ms. Rainbow slightly. "I'll do my best. But I don't know what the Association will say."

"Inspector!" Harrison yelped. She was pointing wildly in the direction of the road. "They're taking the car away."

Across the park, the blue and white was being winched aboard a tow truck, to the cheers of a group of placard-bearing adults. Needless to say this impromptu act of rebellion was attended by several television crews.

"Oh shit." Yelling at Harrison to call for backup, Amanda started running.

So, the situation was in hand, huh? Hadn't they

said that about Somalia, too? Amanda glanced around as a male voice accosted her.

"Welcome back, Inspector!" Rodney McInnes, a pest from Radio New Zealand News, waved eagerly from the branch of a tree. "How was New York?"

"A cultural experience," Amanda panted. "You should try it sometime."

McInnes haw-hawed as he grappled his way down the tree trunk, landing virtually on top of a woman protester. Without so much as an apology, he pushed through the crowd, hurling questions at Amanda.

"How many kids are missing, Inspector? Have any bodies been recovered so far?"

Before she could tell him to butt out, he had already begun his radio spiel. ". . . live from the grisly investigation into a suspected child abduction ring in the Aro Valley. Detective Inspector Amanda Valentine is with me at the moment. Any suspects, Inspector?"

"There are no details available at this time."

"Is kiddy porn involved?"

"Mr. McInnes —" Amanda got no further. Sirens howling, tires squealing, several patrol cars converged on the scene. Harrison, managing to locate a loud hailer, began shouting instructions to the crowd to disperse.

A scruffy man wearing a Men for Non-Violence lapel button and pushing twins in a stroller, shoved past Amanda.

"Gilbert!" a woman shouted and pointed. "It's her. The Police Inspector."

The man turned. "I hope you're satisfied," he snarled at Amanda. "If you people were reasonable, if you —"

He uttered a startled gasp as Amanda seized his arm. "You're under arrest, Mr. Friend," she said. "For organizing an unlawful assembly." As the cameras rolled she handcuffed him and frog-marched him to a car.

"But my children! What about my sons?"

"Read him his rights," Amanda instructed a constable. "And fetch his sons. They're the ugly ones in the pink stroller."

The media tailed her to Police Headquarters where they joined a crush of reporters clamoring on the front steps. Thankful for the underground entrance, Amanda bailed out of her car and slammed the door.

Taking several deep calming breaths, she rode the elevator to her office and hung out a Meeting in Progress sign. Sitting at her desk, watching the message light on her panel blink, she rested her chin on her arms and imagined someone holding her.

It was nearly eighteen months since the end of her relationship with Debby Daley. Since then, she had had the occasional fling. Nothing serious, complicated, unsettling, thrilling. No one who could make her stomach roll and her common sense depart.

And probably a good thing. Hers was the kind of job that lovers found hard to accept. They couldn't compete with a beeper sounding at midnight. They couldn't depend on anything — a dinner plan, a weekend away, a partner's undivided attention. Did it have to be that way? Amanda wondered. It must be possible to find someone who would not have unrealistic expectations. Sure, a small voice jibed, a doormat.

Amanda watched a gull hovering outside her window, riding the breeze. Thirty-four wasn't so old. There were plenty of singles her age. All she had to do was make an effort to meet some of them. Roseanne was always offering to fix her up with a social worker or someone from the Juvenile Courts. Maybe a blind date wasn't such a bad idea.

Her direct line rang. Automatically, Amanda lifted the receiver, muttering, "Valentine."

"Amanda?" a silky unmistakable voice said. "This is Debby."

Amanda could hear her own heart pounding. Morphic resonance. Somehow, Debby had picked up her thoughts.

"I heard you were back," Debby continued. "How are you?"

Flummoxed, Amanda said, "Fine. Busy."

"You're investigating the Sybil Knight murder?"

"News travels."

There was a brief silence. "I'm in Wellington at the moment. I thought we could get together."

"On business or pleasure?" It sounded so much more cynical than she had intended. Amanda could have bitten off her own tongue. Why was she behaving like this? She wanted to see Debby, didn't she? "I'm sorry," she said quickly. "That was a stupid thing to say."

"It's okay." Debby sounded remote. "Maybe this wasn't such a good idea, after all. Anyway —" Her voice took on a hard edge. "Since you asked. It is business. I'm putting something together on the Sybil Knight killing."

Amanda couldn't swallow her anger. "Then you're speaking to the wrong person. Detective Senior Sergeant Shaw is handling media inquiries."

"I see."

For a moment Amanda heard the soft sound of breathing. Then just a curt click.

"We got four TV crews camped out there, ma'am," the Sergeant informed Amanda. "The Chief's wife couldn't get past."

What do you want me to do? Amanda felt like saying.

"DSS Shaw's already seen them. But they insist on talking to you, ma'am. Shall I fob them off with tea and biscuits?"

"Why not throw them a few bones," Amanda muttered.

"Beef bones was it, ma'am?"

"All right Sergeant," Amanda said mildly. "I'll deal with them."

There was nothing to be gained by alienating the news media, she reminded herself as she took the stairs to the press room. She was above the juvenile point-scoring some senior police staff engaged in. Wellington Homicide was the most respected of the CIB divisions in New Zealand. They had the highest clearance rate, the leanest task force, the most visible affirmative action recruitment policies. And she, Amanda Valentine, was the jewel in their crown; the highest ranked senior female detective in New Zealand.

This fact, combined with a certain amount of camera appeal, an exotic accent and a spectacular track record, had established Amanda as a hot media property. Her appearance on *Crimewatch* was guaranteed to lift the ratings, her profile had appeared in every women's magazine, with coy references to her "apparent disinterest in male companionship," and she had received a Royal Honor. She was also a hit with the New Zealand Government, living evidence that no more spending was required on equal opportunity programs. Women only had themselves to blame if they failed to make it to the top of their professions.

Amanda was well aware that her fast-track progress through the CIB ranks and her assignment to glamour cases had started out as a look-good exercise for the Police Department. Many of the senior brass had been quietly confident that she would fold under pressure and provide justification for the continued sidelining of senior women seeking promotion. But it hadn't happened, and as Amanda's reputation had grown, even her fiercest critics had fallen into brooding silence.

Counting slowly to ten, she entered the press room to a barrage of flashes. Diplomatically, she maintained a cool professional smile long enough to satisfy the photographers. "Ladies and gentlemen, thank you for sparing the time for this briefing. I have a short statement to make, then I can take questions."

With some satisfaction she observed bent heads

and pencils flying as she spoke about the Sybil Knight case. Extensive interviews had opened several promising avenues of inquiry, she said. The public had been very forthcoming. An early arrest seemed likely.

"Was this a sex crime, Inspector?" someone called from the back of the room.

"As yet the autopsy findings have not been released," Amanda replied. "So we are unable to determine with any certainty the nature of the assault on Ms. Knight." She selected the waving hand of Suzette Lord, a well-known TV anchor.

"Is the killer a woman?" Suzette demanded.

"At this stage we have not ruled out that possibility."

Naturally the media was agog. An entire ethnic population was being wiped out in Rwanda, men could kill their wives and children every day of the week . . . but a woman involved in what could be a sex killing . . . It was huge.

"The Lynx is a known lesbian club," Suzette Lord was determined to pursue her angle. "Is it possible there is a lesbian killer at large?"

The room fell silent. Television cameras closed in like circling sharks.

"A killer who targets lesbians?" Amanda willfully misunderstood the question. "That's possible. Hate crimes against gay people are rare in New Zealand, but not unheard of."

She was drowned out by the general clamor. Was she saying Sybil Knight was a lesbian?

"I can't comment on that," Amanda said.

What about herself? several opportunists demanded. Her name had been linked with several well known gay and lesbian charities.

"That's probably because I support them, as does the Mayor and many other intelligent public figures." Amanda checked her watch. "I don't have much more time available . . ."

"Can you comment on rumors that Sir George Knight is trying to have the case buried?"

"I'm sure Sir George is as determined as we are that his daughter's killer will be caught," she responded evasively.

A flurry of questions erupted, the press slathering at the mention of that magical name. Sir George Knight was expected to run for parliament in the next elections, speculation about his ambitions recently fueled by his resignation from several company boards and his continuous presence on national television. The death of his daughter in bizarre circumstances could damage hopes of a glittering political career. It was a front-page story.

Acutely conscious that she was skating on thin ice, Amanda drew the press conference to a conclusion, offering as a consolation prize a suitably worded caution. "I'm sure you appreciate that in a crime of this unusual and disturbing nature, we must take care not to inflame public opinion. I will be happy to respond to your questions tomorrow morning, when I'm in a position to comment more fully."

Doing her best to look as though she could hardly wait for the opportunity to deliver on this promise, she moved through a throng of cameras to the exit. As she reached the corridor, someone touched her arm and a breathless voice pleaded, "Inspector . . ."

Turning sharply, her heart leaping into her throat, Amanda met the bright-eyed stare of a young woman fumbling with a microphone. Disappointment welled. She could barely speak, the young woman's question lost somewhere between shock and realization.

She still wanted Debby Daley.

CHAPTER ELEVEN

On her desk was the large white envelope she was waiting for. Amanda withdrew the top sheet. As always Moira's summary was lucid and concise, drawing together the autopsy findings and her own preliminary observations based on the forensic evidence gathered.

Sybil Knight had died of a brain hemorrhage approximately half an hour after being knocked unconscious by a blow to the back of the skull. The weapon was thought to be a solid object, possibly a brick. No traces of masonry were found in her hair or in the depression itself, so it was possible the weapon had been wrapped in cloth. Time of death was estimated at between 02:30 — 03:00 a.m.

Bodily injuries were superficial and appeared to have been inflicted while she was unconscious. No evidence of sexual assault. A termination of pregnancy had occurred within the preceding week.

Amanda's head swam. An abortion? She checked the name on the autopsy to be certain it was Sybil Knight's. Perspiration damped her forehead. Sybil had been pregnant. Amanda could barely take it in. Kim Curtis had said nothing about baby plans.

Even as she thought it, Amanda deplored her own naivete. As a homicide detective, she harbored few illusions about human behavior. Consequently she was seldom surprised in any investigation. Disgusted, yes. Appalled and depressed, yes. People were, she reflected grimly, capable of almost anything.

She paced across her office and leaned against the window frame, allowing her thoughts to roam. Either Sybil Knight had been raped or she had been having an affair with a man. She had become pregnant and had had an abortion. In her diary on the Friday before her death, she had likened her feelings to waking from a bad dream. Thank God for Marlene, she had written.

Recalling the psychiatrist's evasiveness, Amanda whispered, "I could kick your butt."

Austin Shaw displayed rare excitement. "Pregnant! Well, that rather throws the cat among the pigeons."

Amanda paced, hands in her pockets. "If she'd

been raped, someone would have known, even if she hadn't reported it. So, she was having an affair. Someone who loved her found out. She was hit over the head and slapped around. It's possible her death was an accident."

"You think her partner did it to teach her a lesson?" He seemed to be having as much difficulty as Amanda, trying to envisage Kim Curtis caning her lover's helpless body.

"We can't rule it out," Amanda said. "And Kim isn't the only suspect. Casey Randall was Sybil's lover before Kim. She concealed the fact in questioning."

"So she wanted Sybil back only to find she was having an affair with a man?" Shaw found the obvious hole in the reasoning. "Why implicate herself by killing Sybil at the club?"

Amanda felt queasy. She wanted an espresso and something chocolatey. Comfort food. "Okay, second possibility — the man she had the affair with killed her — who knows what reason. Maybe she dumped him, maybe he wanted the kid. I'm convinced the guy was stalking her. From all accounts she was a nervous wreck."

"So she couldn't tell anyone what was going on, without revealing what she had done," Shaw observed. "We are, of course, assuming the stalker and the killer are one in the same."

"It seems likely," Amanda said, calling to mind a long list of homicides carried out by obsessed men who stalked previous partners.

"I'm not convinced," Shaw said.

"You think she had an enemy?" Amanda said. "Todd Parker-Brown is an asshole but I don't think he's our man. He's too obvious about loathing her."

"Which leaves a fourth possibility — an opportunist killing," Shaw surmised. "A stranger encounters her in the night."

"Why would a stranger steal her MIL key and enter the Gallery? The killer must have wanted something that was in there. Something that would connect him, or her, to the crime." Amanda pictured Sybil leaving the club and walking to the Gallery. The killer must have been watching her, waiting for her. "Besides, a stranger-crime would probably have involved a sexual attack. I think we can rule out that theory."

"The statistics favor your second guess," Shaw commented. "And murder is a man's crime."

"With most of the victims the women they claim to love. Curious way of showing it."

Shaw did not blink. "So, we find all the men who loved Sybil."

For a moment Amanda contemplated this. "I think it's time we got an expert opinion on our theories," she remarked dryly. "I'm going to go see if there's anything else Dr. Friedman overlooked telling me yesterday. Get Jonathan Knight in here. I'll talk to him when I get back."

"Is that entirely wise?" Shaw was guarded. "The Knights are very clear about wanting to keep a low profile."

Amanda quirked an eyebrow. "He doesn't have to come through the front doors," she said softly.

Marlene Friedman had a client with her.

"I'll wait," Amanda said.

The psychiatrist looked at her sharply. "Why don't we set an appointment time? My client has just arrived."

"This is urgent." Amanda took a pace forward, compelling Marlene to step aside. "May I come in?"

Marlene's expression was taut with temper and disbelief. Obviously she was not used to obeying anyone's commands. Leading Amanda to a brightly decorated studio adjoining the kitchen, she said in a rapid undertone, "I don't know what this intrusion is about, Inspector, but I am offended by your behavior."

"Then we have something in common," Amanda said tersely.

"I'll see if my client is able to return at another time." Marlene swept from the room, leaving her distinctive perfume.

Restlessly, Amanda wandered from the studio to the kitchen. The area was cheerful, very modern. If Marlene had decorated her house herself, it revealed a pragmatic nature and a liking for comfort without clutter.

A curving window faced onto the front of the house. Drawn to it, Amanda idly gazed out. Marlene's home was deceptively plain in appearance, its white concrete walls suggesting a cold modernity belied by the interior. The only sign of an occupant was a small rack of women's shoes beside the doorstep. Marlene Friedman did not subscribe to burglar deterrents like a pair of huge men's working boots and a faux guard dog door alarm.

At the sound of voices, Amanda retreated from

the window, mentally composing her questions. Marlene Friedman had concealed important information about Sybil. Some cops would call that obstructing an investigation.

She watched Marlene exchanging a few words with her client at the front door, and with a faint start, recognized the slender sandy-haired man. David Jordan, Sybil's friend from the support group.

As he strolled off, Marlene entered the kitchen. "You're alone today, Inspector?" She ushered Amanda into the large sitting room overlooking the sea and gestured toward a soft armchair.

"That's right."

"Isn't that contrary to your usual practice?"

Amanda gave a noncommittal shrug. Placing her tape recorder on a low table nearby, she asked. "Do you mind?"

"I'm sure it would make no difference if I did." Marlene sat down and crossed her legs. "Perhaps you could tell me what this is about?"

"I believe you have withheld information significant to this investigation," Amanda said. "Did you know Sybil Knight was pregnant?"

Marlene's expression barely altered. "I knew," she said.

"You failed to tell me."

"It was a private matter. I had promised Sybil I would never discuss it with anyone."

Amanda bit back the retort that sprang to her lips — that she was sure Sybil would find that a big help. Forcing an even tone, she said, "It's a little late to be concerned about Sybil's privacy now. Thanks to your peculiar brand of ethics, I've lost valuable time in this investigation. Do you think you can manage to answer my questions today, Doctor?"

Marlene Friedman smoothed her dark plait. "It was never my intention to mislead you, Inspector."

Amanda read this as cooperation. "Did you help arrange an abortion for Sybil?"

"Yes."

"When and where was that carried out?"

"At the Parkview Clinic on Friday last week." Marlene avoided Amanda's eyes. She seemed on the brink of tears.

"Who knew about this?"

"No one."

"Not even Kim?"

"Sybil didn't tell anyone. She said the affair was a terrible mistake. She wanted to put it behind her and start again."

"How far advanced was the pregnancy?"

"Ten weeks."

Amanda tried to imagine living with a woman and failing to notice that she had missed two periods in a row. It was possible, she supposed, if you weren't having much of a sex life.

"Who was the father?"

"I don't know. Sybil never spoke about him."

"Did he know she was pregnant?"

"I don't think so. Sybil was no longer seeing him when she found out. She was trying very hard to sort out her relationship with Kim and make a success of her new job."

And was prepared to live a lie in order to do it, Amanda thought. "Do you know anything at all about the man she was seeing?"

"I saw Sybil the day she broke off the affair. He had taken it badly. He was much more involved than she was, you see."

"Sybil was not in love with him?"

"Sybil was experimenting. Many people do — gay and straight. Of course there's an enormous amount of denial."

Amanda paused to gather her thoughts. "So, are you saying Sybil was confused about her sexuality?"

"Unresolved," Marlene corrected. "Sybil knew she was lesbian, but she seemed to have an overwhelming need to verify it. This meant she had many relationships with women, and eventually she experimented with a man as well."

Big mistake. Amanda spoke her thoughts. "And the guy got serious?"

"I gather he could not take no for an answer," Marlene affirmed. "Sybil saw him several times to try and talk it through."

"But you have no idea who he is."

"You've asked me that several times, Inspector." Marlene was cool and direct. "Do you think I'm lying?"

Amanda conceded the point with a wry nod. "I'm sorry. It's just how we do things." And, she added silently, I'm worried that I've lost my touch and I'll miss some vital clue. "Is there anything else you think I should know about Sybil?" she asked.

"There is one thing." Marlene was reflective. "She spent three months in a mental hospital when she was fifteen, after an attempted suicide."

"Do you know why she did it?"

"I can't say for certain. There is seldom a simple explanation for suicide. We were gradually working toward dealing with that experience in therapy. I have the hospital records for that period, if you wish to see them." She retrieved a yellow envelope from a file drawer and passed this to Amanda. "They're not very helpful. Sexist assumptions masquerading as psychoanalysis."

"Do you have a theory of your own?"

"I try not to theorize," Marlene said. "It's always so tempting to arrange the facts to fit."

CHAPTER TWELVE

Despite his professed indignation at being brought to the Station in the middle of a business day, Jonathan Knight emanated a smothered excitement. Pointedly standing until Amanda was seated, he said with prep school pomposity, "I hope you have a very good reason for calling me here, Inspector."

"I do." Amanda left him to draw his own conclusions, inquiring, "Coffee?"

"No thank you. I've just dined." With apparent discomfort, he watched Austin Shaw pour a cup and hand it to Amanda. Roles, it seemed, were clearly defined in Jonathan Knight's world. Men did not serve the coffee except in restaurants, where they were paid to.

As Amanda took her seat, he followed suit, leaning slightly toward her, his hands on the small table between them. His gaze was intense and speculative.

"I'm glad you were able to come in, Mr. Knight," Amanda said pleasantly.

"It seemed appropriate. Detective Shaw was quite right. Some matters are best avoided around a lady of my mother's sensibilities."

Amanda held back a groan. "I have to ask some difficult questions, Mr. Knight," she said diplomatically. "Please speak frankly. I'm aware of Sybil's lifestyle."

His mouth tightened with distaste. "You and everyone else. God knows she advertised it."

The women in Jonathan Knight's life belonged on pedestals, Amanda deduced. And he was outraged that Sybil had abandoned hers. "You sound angry with your sister."

"Wouldn't you be? Sybil had a great future. We had to sit back and watch her risk everything for some kind of warped rebellion against the values she grew up with."

He seemed even further to the right than his parents, Amanda marveled. "In your earlier statement, you said you arrived home from a trip to Auckland on Monday night at nine and went directly to your apartment where you stayed. According to one of your neighbors, this is not so. You were seen driving from your building at one-thirty in the morning."

Apparently Jonathan believed attack to be the best form of defense. Red-faced, he demanded, "What are you getting at? You think I had something to do with my sister's murder?"

"Did you?"

Jonathan got to his feet. "This is outrageous. I came here to help."

"Then tell me why you went out again on Monday night." Amanda persisted.

"It has nothing to do with you . . . with any of this . . ."

"Mr. Knight, are you aware of the penalties for giving a false statement to the police?"

"Is that supposed to scare me?"

Amanda sighed. "Put yourself in my shoes for a moment, Mr. Knight. I'm looking for a reason Sybil was killed. If I can find it, I have my killer."

"And you think it might be me! I loved my sister. I've never loved anyone the way I loved Syb . . ." Self-consciously, he broke off.

"I understand you and Sybil were very close," Amanda said carefully. "Forgive me for being insensitive."

Apparently mollified, Jonathan returned to his chair. "You're doing your job," he allowed. "God knows I wish you every success. Just give me five minutes with the bastard once you get him. Was she . . ." He studied his white knuckles.

"Sexually assaulted?" Amanda finished his sentence. "I gather not."

"Thank God for that." His voice was fractured. "I couldn't stand that."

His sister was dead and he was worried about whether she had been raped. It was natural, Amanda reminded her cynical self. An untimely death was appalling enough. No one wanted their loved one to have suffered beforehand.

"I went to see her body." He became choked. "I wanted to. She looked just the same. Pale of course, but still . . . Sybil."

Amanda gave him a moment to compose himself. "When you had dinner with Sybil last week, did you notice anything different about her?"

Jonathan squared his jaw, evidently grappling with self-doubt. "I believe so. She seemed extremely nervous."

"This was unusual for Sybil?"

"Very. Normally my sister was a confident person, but she was on edge that evening. Actually I've never seen anything quite like it. She almost jumped out of her chair when the wine waiter opened the champagne."

"Did you ask her what was wrong?"

"She wouldn't tell me," he said bitterly. "Sybil thought I didn't accept who she was. Certainly I didn't agree with her choices, but I loved her anyway. That wasn't good enough for Sybil. I had to love her kinky friends too."

"What do you know about Sybil's relationship with Kim?"

He looked cautious. "I don't think Sybil was happy, if that's what you're asking. In fact I suspect she was finally coming to her senses. Kim Curtis's days were numbered."

"What makes you say that?"

Jonathan was almost cocky. "A couple of months ago Sybil made a new will. She left the house to me."

"I understand you and Sybil had a disagreement over the house."

"No doubt Kim Curtis told you that." Jonathan grunted. "Well maybe you should ask her what she was doing inviting real estate agents to assess the property behind Sybil's back." When Amanda was silent, he went on. "You don't believe me? Ask her. Kim Curtis was with my sister for only one reason. Money."

For a few moments, Amanda watched the second hand progress around her watch, deliberating on Jonathan's resentment of his sister's lover. Returning her attention to the well-dressed man sitting opposite, she said, "Why did your sister attempt suicide when she was fifteen?"

Jonathan shifted in his seat. "How do you know about that?"

"I have the hospital records here." Amanda opened the file and began reading aloud. "*An inappropriate closeness exists between Sybil and her older brother.* What did the doctor mean by that?"

Jonathan's gaze was remote. "The man was an idiot," he said with controlled rage. "He filled Sybil's head with filthy ideas. He desecrated the nature of our relationship."

"How would you describe that nature, Mr. Knight?"

"We had a perfect love. Innocent and trusting. We were brother and sister, for God's sake." He glared, suddenly the child confronting hostile adults.

"Yet Sybil wanted to die," Amanda said softly. "She must have been terribly unhappy about something."

"She was," Jonathan said grimly. "I suppose that

was when it all began, really. She had this thing for a teacher and knowing how sick it was, she tried to get over it, of course. That only made matters worse and in the end she was so desperate to get this woman's attention, she took an overdose."

Amanda could barely frame her thoughts into a sentence. She had heard enough, she decided. "Returning to Monday night," she said. "Where were you from one until four?"

Jonathan flicked a glance to Austin Shaw who was leaning against the far wall, apparently preoccupied with his notes. "Very well Inspector. But I want your guarantee that this information will remain within these four walls."

"You're in no position to demand guarantees, Mr. Knight." Amanda got to her feet with a detached attitude. "You are presently without an alibi for the time your sister was killed and you've made a false statement of your whereabouts. That is an offense." Addressing Austin Shaw, she added, "Book him, Shaw —"

"Wait!" Jonathan Knight was on his feet. "This is ridiculous. I was seeing someone . . . a woman . . . that's all."

Amanda continued her progress toward the door. "DSS Shaw will take down her name and address."

"No! You don't understand." His arm jerked out, as if to detain her, but was withdrawn immediately.

Amanda paused, holding the door handle.

"Gina something . . . some French name," Jonathan Knight babbled. "She's a prostitute." He could hardly pronounce the word. "I picked her up in Marion Street."

"Gina . . ." Amanda repeated the name

thoughtfully. It corresponded with recollections of a baby-faced young woman with bleached blonde hair and an ersatz leopard coat. "Did you use a condom?" she asked blandly.

"W . . . what?" Apparently this was another word he couldn't say.

Meeting his nonplussed stare, she explained, "Gina la Petite is HIV positive."

CHAPTER THIRTEEN

On her way home, Amanda collected a burger and stopped by the Prostitutes' Collective. The organization was housed in a grotty little building on Cuba Street, its doors and windows plastered in safe sex literature.

As Amanda entered, a statuesque woman, apparently engaged in telephone counseling, blew her a kiss and indicated a seat. "Lovie," she dulcetly advised her caller, "it's a raid. Excuse me while I show the officer some hospitality." Extravagant lashes swept up and Amanda felt herself thoroughly assessed.

"About five-nine," the woman spoke into the phone, "Hunky, nearly blonde, grey eyes. Definitely works out." Placing a perfunctory hand over the receiver, she explained to Amanda, "Uniform junkie."

Amanda poured herself some aging Kona coffee and sat down in the meeting-room-cum-office to enjoy her half-cold burger. Despite the radiant heater blazing in one corner, the room was so cold she kept her coat on. Wincing at the rough flavor of the coffee, she flicked through the latest copy of *Siren,* the prostitutes' newsletter.

In Wellington, the cops now made an effort to get on with the local sex workers. This spirit of cooperation was a new strategy which paid dividends on both sides. When the cops wanted information, they generally got it, and when a working girl laid a complaint it generally resulted in a prosecution. This hadn't always been the case.

When Amanda had first joined the CIB, six years before, relations were frosty. To get the quality of information she was looking for, she had made it her business to cultivate contacts among the street-walkers. One of these, a transvestite named Jezebel Matenga, now described herself as a sexual health counselor. A plaque bearing this legend was nailed above the cluttered desk where she carried out her volunteer work for the Collective.

Finally dropping the phone into its cradle, Jezebel lifted frosted apricot nails to her bouffant hair and released a protracted sigh. "His boyfriend's had him in a long-line panty-girdle for the past two years. He's getting so much traffic he's ex-hausted, poor boy." She examined her face in a hand-mirror, replenished her lipstick, then turned her attention to Amanda. "Now then, lovie. What can this old queen do for you?"

Amanda finished the awful coffee. "Seen Gina la Petite recently?"

"What's that girl done now? The young are such a trial."

"She's someone's alibi."

Jezebel rolled her eloquent brown eyes. "Well, don't tell her that. She'll charge by the minute." She sashayed across the room to a filing cabinet, a vision in orange chiffon bell bottoms, a lime halter top, matching lime platforms and a purple satin jacket.

"Nice outfit," Amanda remarked.

"You too. Get that coat in New York?"

Nodding, Amanda fingered her extravagant purchase. A cashmere and lambswool mix, it was an indulgence — the financially catastrophic consequences of having too much time on her hands.

"You on that S/M business at the Lynx?" Jezebel passed her a card on which she had written Gina's contact details. "Dreadful, just dreadful. But you can't tell an amateur how to play safe, lovie. They hand their brains in at the door."

"You know the Lynx?"

"Sure do. Some of the girls got a burlesque act going down there. Nice place."

Amanda was a little surprised. Most of the lesbian joints about town had a strict women-only policy which included live entertainment. She had assumed the Lynx to be the same, but clearly Casey Randall enjoyed stepping on politically correct toes. She chewed relentlessly on her burger, attempting to identify the flavor of the meat. It felt like rubbery beef but it tasted like a weird cross between pork and venison. The packaging featured a large map of Australia behind a red kangaroo.

"You get that down the road at Ozzie's?" Jezebel asked. "Can't say it appeals — roo-burger. He does snake and crocodile, too."

"I'll remember that," Amanda said.

At home, Amanda lay on her sofa unable to concentrate on anything except the silence of the house. She had always lived alone, and that was how she liked it. If she wanted company, she could go out. If she wanted a lover, she could find one.

It was natural, she supposed, that approaching her mid-thirties a woman was bound to reflect on how she had spent her twenties and to wonder what she would do for the rest of her life. Some women panicked in the face of this fathomless future. Some got religion or stopped smoking or had a baby or an affair. Like Sybil.

Amanda tried to imagine her house filled with life. Music, voices, the smell of food, the phone ringing, doors opening and shutting, the traffic of feet, clothes piled high on the washing machine, a dog chasing Madam.

Her eyes stung. She had never experienced anything like that, not even in childhood. Why should she miss it now?

Calling Madam, she gathered the little cat to her breasts. For some inexplicable reason, she felt sad and terribly tired. It was one of those days when the world felt like a hopeless mess, people struggling to make any sense out of it. Little wonder the religious right was so attractive to so many people, she reflected. It must be a relief to switch off your brain, to abrogate personal responsibility, to employ dogma to shore up prejudice and justify scapegoating.

Snap out of it, Amanda told herself. Wallowing in existential angst would bring her no closer to a cooked meal. Nuzzling Madam, she got up and padded to the kitchen, For a moment the spotless benchtops defeated her. As a child it had been her great ambition to bring a friend home to a cozy house with food cooking on the stove, jars of pickles in cupboards, a mother in an apron. Instead, twice a week, she had journeyed from Queens to Manhattan, to share takeout food with her mother, who, while delighted to see her, didn't seem sure what to do with her.

Amanda knew now that it had made sense for her parents to separate. Theirs was a teen romance which had led to an unwanted pregnancy — Amanda — and an unhappy marriage. Eventually they had faced up to reality. They had nothing in common except their child, and they both wanted more out of life than a loveless farce of a marriage could provide. They had parted as friends when Amanda was eleven, her father offering to take custody of Amanda so that her mother could complete school.

Somehow the arrangement had continued and Amanda had never lived with her mother again. It was not until Kelly came along, when Amanda was a rookie cop in her Dad's precinct, that Amanda got to have her cozy kitchen and jars of pickles. That had been twelve years ago — a life so distant it seemed unreal.

Struck by a glaring longing for what was lost, Amanda leaned against the barren benchtop and closed her eyes. Get over it, she told herself.

CHAPTER FOURTEEN

Moira McDougall's office would have looked like anyone else's but for her cherished collection of preserved body parts. A peculiar breed of trophy, these occupied a large display case on one wall. As always, Amanda's eyes were drawn to the discreetly labeled jars.

"The eye is new," Moira informed her, as a doll collector might vaunt a recent acquisition. "Intriguing case — the Kensington Court rapist."

Amanda had read the file when she returned from

New York. A woman had killed her rapist in self defense, blinding him with a spray deodorant during the struggle. The prosecution had argued that once sightless, he was disabled and there was no further argument for self-defense. It had been for Moira to establish the extent and duration of his temporary blindness. Her evidence had favored the defense and the woman was acquitted.

"Sybil Knight . . ." Amanda prompted.

Moira held aloft a dense file. "We have a way to go, yet. But there is some good news. We took saliva samples from the face, neck, breasts and stomach. I'll have the first test results from serology by tomorrow."

"He licked her?"

"Or kissed her," Moira suggested.

"Semen?" Sybil had not been raped, but that did not rule out the possibility that her killer had ejaculated elsewhere.

Moira discounted this possibility. "We've checked every square inch of the place. There was nothing on the victim's clothing, either." She adjusted her glasses and located a summary written in her characteristic turquoise script. "As you can imagine, the trace has been a challenge. This is a nightclub — hordes of people tramping through. Luckily the crime and our sampling occurred within the same period of closure."

Hair and fibers taken from inside the back entrance indicated that Sybil had lain on the carpet there, Moira said. "He brought her in through the back door, left her on the floor while he closed it, lifted her and carried her upstairs to the room in which she was found. While she was unconscious, he removed her clothes and handcuffed her."

"The beating? She was unconscious?"

"There was no evidence of self-defense or struggle. Her facial injuries were consistent with punches and slaps. Her back..." Moira was reflective. "We identified the cane used. It had been returned to a rack on the wall."

"Prints?"

"A nightmare. Card a suspect and we can look for a match."

"Do you have any sense of him?" Amanda asked.

As always, the pathologist was reluctant to embark on what she described as unscientific speculation, reminding Amanda, "I'm no profiler."

"Observations..." Amanda fished. "Intuition..."

"There is something." Moira closed Sybil Knight's file. "Purely a matter of common sense. I'm convinced the caning was an afterthought."

Amanda had drawn the same conclusion. Beating an unconscious woman hardly seemed a genuine sadist's idea of fun.

"It's possible that he did not set out to kill her," Moira said. "He knocked her unconscious. If he had simply wanted to kill her, he could have achieved it on the spot and made his escape. Instead he removed her to that particular room. Why?"

"To throw us off the scent," Amanda suggested. "Or maybe to frame someone." If the killer had hoped to make the crime resemble a bondage scene, it was an amateurish attempt.

"Perhaps." Moira seemed to share her

reservations. "My guess is revenge. He wanted to punish her for something."

"So he leaves her in a dungeon at a lesbian club. His idea of humiliation."

"And having rendered her naked and vulnerable, he feels powerful," Moira continued reflectively.

Amanda imagined the faceless assailant standing over his victim. Had he wanted her to plead in terror wondering what he was going to do to her? If so, he must have planned to kill her, rather than leave her alive to identify him. "When he couldn't rouse her, he struck her face," she conjectured. It was consistent with her facial bruising.

"If he had not planned to kill her, he may have panicked at that point," Moira advanced her theory. "He then seized a cane and beat her. Possibly out of rage and frustration. Or perhaps, as you say, he wanted to disguise his crime as some kind of sadomasochistic scene."

"You're certain it was a man?" Amanda asked. The question seemed almost redundant. Murders of this type were seldom committed by women.

"Serology may prove me wrong, but at the moment I'm assuming so. Whoever it was had to be strong enough to carry her up those stairs."

Amanda was silent. He had waited for Sybil, she thought. One quick crushing blow to the back of her head and she was unconscious. "The parking lot. He must have attacked her there," she said.

Only it didn't quite add up. Casey Randall claimed to have driven off at twenty minutes past two. Sybil had already left the Gallery by then and would have been walking back along Harris Street. Why hadn't Casey seen her? Had the attack occurred outside the Gallery?

That seemed improbable. Would any perpetrator in his right mind knock a woman unconscious only yards away from Police Headquarters and then carry her body all the way to the Lynx? Even if he had, the entrance to the Police Station's underground parking was on Harris Street. Patrol cars were constantly arriving or departing. He would have been seen.

"There were no signs of a forced entry at the Lynx," Amanda said, uneasy at the ramifications.

Moira stated the obvious. "Perhaps he had a key,"

Amanda found herself shaking her head, completely rejecting the idea that Casey Randall could be lying, that it could have been Casey who had lain in wait for Sybil.

But if the killer didn't have a key, how did he, or she, gain access to the Lynx?

Amanda put the same question to her investigating team at the morning's briefing.

"The guy used her MIL key to gain entry to the Gallery, didn't he?" one detective noted. "Maybe the victim also had a key to the club and this fell into the perpetrator's hands."

"Or it was the Randall woman." Detective Sergeant Solomon, who had recently joined some fundamentalist church, was convinced of Casey's guilt.

Ownership of a lesbian club was surely all the evidence they needed. The devil had that woman in his sights.

"There is another possibility," Austin Shaw politely suggested. "Perhaps he was already inside the club. That might explain how he knew the location of the dungeon."

He offered a thumbnail reconstruction. The killer crept in the front door as Casey was going through the building closing up. The lights were out. There were plenty of places to hide. As soon as Casey had left, he headed for the back door, unbolting it and wedging it open. Then he waited behind the glass recycling drums in the parking lot. As Sybil unlocked her car, he struck her over the head.

"Sybil left the Gallery at two-eighteen, but Casey didn't see her returning to the Lynx," Amanda pointed out. "So where was she?"

"We got something on that," Detective Nikora contributed. "Bunch of street kids in Civic Square said a lady fitting the description gave them some money that night. Couldn't say what time, but they blew it at the pie cart on Courtenay Place. The guy on the cart said they showed up around quarter to three."

"So Sybil walked through Civic Square instead of taking the Harris Street route." Amanda felt like kicking herself. Had her brain calcified while she was on leave?

"Which means Casey Randall could have left the club at twenty past two without seeing her," Shaw said. "We haven't had much luck verifying what time

Ms. Randall arrived home. She's always late, so the neighbors don't pay much attention."

"Who else is unaccounted for?" Amanda asked.

Jonathan Knight's alibi checked out, Solomon sonorously declared. Miss Gina La Petite had phoned through a credit card transaction in his name just after two in the morning. He had left the hotel room about an hour later.

Kim Curtis claimed she was asleep in bed. The nearest neighbor did not hear a car leaving or arriving at any time that night. Marlene Friedman had taken an emergency call from a depressed client at two-thirty. This checked out.

Sybil's parents had attended a July 4 celebration at the residence of the United States Ambassador. Their chauffeur had collected them at one-thirty and they arrived at their home at one-forty-five. They did not use the car again that night. Their security system was fully activated, and had remained so until six in the morning.

Amanda moved to the huge white board. "The killer is somewhere on this board." There were about twenty names in all, with a brief description of their relationship to Sybil and their whereabouts at the time of the killing.

"We're going to go through these names one by one and examine the information we have about each individual and interview them again if necessary. We are looking for a man with whom Sybil had a brief sexual relationship. We are also looking for Sybil's Filofax and her MIL security key." She turned to Shaw. "How did you get on with Sybil's doctor?"

135

"They have no record of her pregnancy diagnosis. The nurse seemed to think she may have had the test done elsewhere, especially if she wanted an abortion referral. I'm checking the Family Planning Clinics this afternoon."

"Parkview?" Amanda glanced at the two detectives she had despatched to the abortion clinic. Bergman and Brody shuffled awkwardly. "We're trying again later today, ma'am," said Bergman, the more seasoned of the two. "Had a slight problem yesterday afternoon."

"A problem?"

"Protesters, ma'am. Wouldn't let us through. We were in a mufti car. They must have thought we were..." He glanced at his companion. Detective Constable Brody, a newly divorced woman in her late twenties who had recently been promoted from the provinces, was gazing at the floor.

"You were mistaken for clients?" Amanda deduced.

"We couldn't get a word in," Bergman said. "They held hands in a circle with us in the middle and started praying — all this stuff about the soul of the little innocent baby we were about to murder... And well... DC Brody got upset and..."

Brody got to her feet, white-faced. "I punched a man, Inspector."

Amanda counted to three. "You did what?"

"I lost my temper, ma'am. DC Bergman had nothing to do with it. I hit the guy."

In another life Amanda would have congratulated her. Instead she was staring disciplinary action in the face. "You hit him. Then what?"

Bergman intervened. "The guy attacked Brody, Inspector. He was screaming at her and these women

136

started hitting us with their handbags... What choice did we have?"

"You made arrests?" Amanda felt weak.

"I'm afraid not, ma'am. We scarpered." As Nikora emitted a strangled giggle, Bergman glanced around his twitchy colleagues, adding sharply, "It wasn't funny."

With a cutting look at Nikora, Brody said, "I take full responsibility ma'am."

"Tell me something," Amanda said mildly. "How were you mistaken for clients?"

"They came straight after us," Brody replied. "We didn't even get a chance to identify ourselves."

Amanda smiled. "I was hoping you would say that." Tucking her notebook into her jacket pocket, she ordered Brody and Bergman to get into uniform, arrange a mufti car and meet her out front in fifteen minutes.

"As for the rest of you," she addressed her team, "I want this case cleared. It's Sybil Knight's funeral this weekend and I want her killer behind bars when they lower that coffin."

A woman with short dark hair and a familiar teasing smile was waiting in Amanda's office. "Don't sack the Sergeant," she said, uncrossing her legs and standing up. "I talked my way in."

I'm sure you did, Amanda thought. She took in Debby's black pleated mini skirt, clinging sweater and melting blue eyes. Like no one else, Debby Daley had always been able to insinuate herself into Amanda's space. "What are you doing here?" she asked.

"I wanted to see you."

"About the Sybil Knight case?"

"That was hurt feelings talking," Debby said softly.

Realizing she was hovering in her own doorway, Amanda entered her room properly, claiming it. "How long are you here for?" She pitched for a conversational tone, fixing her gaze on a point slightly to one side of Debby's head.

"A few more days." Debby perched guilelessly on the edge of Amanda's desk. "I've missed you."

"You've changed your perfume." Amanda distanced herself from the memories — her sheets smelling of Obsession, traces lingering on her clothing and car upholstery. Was Debby similarly haunted?

"You have to try something different occasionally." Debby extended her wrist. "It's Cartier. Do you like it?"

Amanda inhaled slightly. The scent was very warm, a little spicy. Debby's skin looked as smooth as butter. "I have an appointment," she said.

"Why are you angry with me?" Debby's eyes were bright, a little reckless, her head cocked in studied appeal.

Resolutely Amanda lifted her file box from her desk and gathered up her coat. "I'm not angry. Just busy."

"I don't understand your behavior," Debby protested, hands on hips. "We had some fun and we said goodbye. It's not as if we were in love!"

Amanda felt as if she had dined on gravel. "We could have been." If either of us had the guts, she added silently.

CHAPTER FIFTEEN

The Parkview Clinic was tucked well out of public view in a tatty building behind the Women's Hospital in Newtown. Its flaking paint, cracked window panes and trampled shrubbery bore testimony to years of budgetary neglect. Lack of parking compelled most clients to run a gamut of anti-choice protestors en route to the front entrance, their destination increasingly obvious as they passed the only other buildings in the vicinity.

Instructing Brody to park discreetly, Amanda appraised the twenty or so protestors gathered beneath umbrellas in the public area. The majority were men, some very young. The handful of women present wore pastel-colored dresses and stood, clearly shivering, in damp stockings and high heels. A variety of signs declared abortion to be a sin and implored expectant mothers to give life to their babies.

Ordering Brody and Bergman to observe from the car until she signaled them, Amanda buttoned her coat and started up the steep path toward the clinic. Within moments she was spotted and the protestors descended toward her, singing "Amazing Grace." A short, balding man with strange bug eyes blocked her path, blazing righteous contempt. There was something familiar about him, but Amanda could not put a finger on it.

"I'm here in the name of Jesus Christ Our Lord," he shouted as the singing dwindled to a tuneless hum.

"You are blocking a public pathway," Amanda said. "Please permit me to pass."

The group immediately joined hands, surrounding her as she continued to walk toward the clinic.

"Let us pray," the short man instructed. "Let us plead for the soul of this innocent child about to be torn from the womb of his mother. Oh Lord, please shine your holy light upon this woman and guide her from this evil path —"

Amanda halted, glancing back toward Bergman and Brody and palming her identification. "Excuse me," she cut sternly across the prayers. "I demand that you let me by immediately."

Ignoring her, the group closed in until Amanda

could feel the brush of their coats, their palpable hatred. She could hardly bear to imagine how a woman might feel, in whatever circumstances had led to the difficult decision to end a pregnancy, to find herself faced with this additional ordeal. Careful not to use any force, she tried to move past the barrier formed by their bodies. Elbows and jostling prevented her gaining ground, and the prayer leader redoubled his efforts.

She would burn in hell for the murder of her tiny baby, he assured her, but there was still time for her soul to be saved. "Turn back!" he shouted, inches from her face.

From somewhere in the small crowd a male voice added, "Whore!" Others began chanting, "Shame on you."

As the verbal abuse rapidly reached a crescendo, and the jostling gave way to small, sharp shoves and kicks, Amanda felt herself perspiring, a coil of fear unwinding in her gut. There was something very disturbing about the pack mentality, in any manifestation. As a cop she had confronted fear almost every day of her career, yet she had seldom felt so threatened. With a hand that shook slightly, she extracted her identification and shoved it in front of their hate-filled faces, shouting, "Police. Step back right now."

The frenzied chanting tapered off to a hostile silence, the protestors falling back a few paces.

"Who is in charge of this group?" Amanda demanded.

After a brief hesitation, the short man announced with bellicose confidence, "We are here in the name

141

of Our Lord. To exercise our right to gather in peaceful protest." He dropped to his knees and began to pray.

Several of the group promptly followed suit. The others gazed uncertainly at the wet paving. What had been light drizzle was now rain.

"You are obstructing a public thoroughfare and creating a traffic hazard." Amanda extracted her notebook and raised an arm, signaling for Brody and Bergman to approach. "Do you have a permit for this gathering?"

"We answer to only one authority," a spotty young man announced. "The highest authority of all . . ."

"You can tell that to the judge," Amanda said coldly. "I'm placing all of you under arrest. You are charged with unlawful assembly and it is likely you will also be cited for gender discrimination, sexual harassment —"

"Slut!" A woman to one side of her spat.

Icy with anger, Amanda wiped a glob of saliva from her cheek, then seized the woman's arm. Twisting it deftly behind her back, she lowered her into a shallow puddle, and holding her firmly, shouted, "Sit down, all of you, hands on your heads. Or you will be charged with resisting arrest."

With a nod at Brody and Bergman, she moved away to the pavement, allowing the young detectives to take over. Thunder rumbled in the distance.

"It's going to pour any minute," Brody commented, examining the heavy sky with a trace of consternation.

Amanda glanced at the bedraggled and squirming

142

protestors. "I guess God looks after his own," she said.

Although she had to pass by home to change into dry clothing, Amanda managed to be on time for lunch with Roseanne. They had arranged to meet at the City Bistro, the trendy restaurant adjoining the Gallery.

"You must be out of your mind." Roseanne scooped the foam from her cappucino into her mouth. "Look at you, for God's sake! Are you a happy and satisfied woman? I don't think so."

"I didn't expect to feel like this." Amanda resentfully daubed at her eyes. She was almost crying. This was a nightmare.

"Oh I see. The wayward girlfriend comes crawling back and the strong silent cop just climbs aboard her Harley and rides into the sunset saying 'Too late baby — you blew it.'" Roseanne sipped at her milkshake. "Grow up, for godssake. You can't play chicken with feelings."

"I don't want to get involved with anyone."

Roseanne looked as if she wanted to slap her. "You're lonely —" She held up her hands as Amanda started to object. "No! Listen to me. I'm your friend. I've noticed. You are lonely and depressed. You're cutting yourself off from people."

Amanda's throat felt sore. "I don't have the energy for a relationship, Rosy. I've been away for a year and I need to get back into my work. I don't need the distraction."

"The distraction..." Roseanne chewed that one over for a moment. "Is that what happened with Debby? You got distracted? I don't think so. I think you got frightened. You lost control, and you hate that, don't you?"

Amanda felt anger stir. "You've taken too many psych classes," she said.

"I don't need to take a class to see what's happening with you, Amanda. You're not unique. Lots of people are scared of making a commitment."

Amanda finished her coffee. "We should stop this conversation while we're still friends." She tried to make it sound flippant, but her voice was too hoarse.

Roseanne was unfazed. Working with street kids, she recognized bravado when she saw it. "See," she challenged gently. "You're doing it to me, too — freezing me out."

Amanda was silent. Intellectually, she could see exactly what her friend was talking about. After Kelly had died, Amanda had not had a relationship for nearly two years. When she finally did, her girlfriends came second to her work. They were nice to have, but she dropped them if they got in the way.

"It's easier to let women go, if I never get close to them," Amanda reflected aloud.

"Who says you have to let them go?" Roseanne asked.

"Look, I know you think this all comes back to Kelly. But I've dealt with it, Roseanne. My lover was killed because I'm a cop. It happens. The truth is it's impossible to mix a job like mine with a great relationship — they're mutually exclusive."

Roseanne silently contemplated the menu board.

144

Frustration was evident in her heightened color and the heave of her small breasts.

"While I was away I found out one really important thing about myself," Amanda continued. "I can survive without a great relationship, but I can't live without the job."

"I see." Roseanne's voice was heavy with irony. "So the kind of woman you are looking for is cute, brainless, undemanding, easily discarded . . . I have the perfect solution."

Seizing Amanda by the arm, she propelled her along Manners Mall to a toy store window display. The sign read LOOK!!! YOUR VERY OWN LIFESIZE BARBIE.

"Very funny," Amanda said.

Roseanne was all innocence. "She'd never dump you."

CHAPTER SIXTEEN

The receptionist on Sybil Knight's floor at the Gallery was a living tribute to Madonna — circa '88. Dressed in black, and rattling with costume jewelry, she disentangled a brown curl from the crucifix in one of her ears, and said, "Hi there, Inspector. The Director says to go on through. If there's anything you need just call me."

"Thanks . . . er . . ." Amanda could not remember the young woman's name. According to the Director, she had been on holiday in Sydney, when Sybil was killed.

"I'm Kylie." She extended a hand. She was wearing white fingerless lace gloves and black nail varnish. "I've seen you on TV."

Amanda took that to mean her competence had been established. Releasing Kylie's hand, she crossed the sapphire-blue carpeting to Sybil's one-time office. The room was sealed. A notice beneath the name plate on the door explained that a police investigation was underway and the room was to be left undisturbed.

Once the case was over, the office would be dismantled, Sybil's belongings crated up and sent to her lover. As if to remove the taint of violent death, management would probably change the furnishings.

It was the third time Amanda had examined Sybil's immediate work environment. Sybil had favored the practical. Her work station was U-shaped, incorporating a desktop and drawers, a set of bookshelves, and a computer. Her desk was piled high with files and paperwork. A slender alarm clock lay face-down in front of her blotter, next to it a small cluster of yellow post-it reminders.

Amanda moved to the door. Signaling the bejeweled receptionist, she asked if the overhead lighting could be turned off for a few minutes. As the room dimmed, she closed the narrow venetian blinds, reducing the light further.

The killer had been in here, she thought, standing in the doorway. Why? Amanda's gaze was drawn to the alarm clock lying face down. Had Sybil knocked it over when she returned to her office that night, or had the subsequent visitor reached for something on the blotter?

Amanda leafed through the clump of post-it notes.

Sybil had been working on her Filofax at this desk, she surmised, and the killer had taken it. Why? What did it contain that linked him or her to the killing?

Amanda moved around the desk. A small waste paper basket was filled to the brim. Austin had already been through it, but Amanda tipped the contents onto the floor anyway. Everything appeared to be work-related. Meeting agendas, lists of tasks to do, reports and drafts of letters.

"Are you okay, Inspector?" The receptionist poked her head around the door. Examining the overturned trash, she said, "Oh dear, can I help you with that?"

Amanda politely declined.

"It's no trouble." Kylie's tone was one of motherly concern. "I know you're a very busy person, and even though it's not my job, I really don't mind a bit. I sometimes acted as PA for Ms. Knight. Did you know that?"

"No, I didn't."

"It was just a private arrangement we had," she confided. "Todd was supposed to help, but you know how it is with men. They don't like a woman in charge."

"What kind of stuff did you do for Ms. Knight?" Amanda made room for the young woman to kneel beside her as they scooped up the rubbish and returned it to Sybil's basket.

"I helped with some of her reports and I looked after her appointments."

"Her appointments?"

"Yeah. She was supposed to have her own secretary like the Director, but there wasn't enough budget left. Todd overspent his allocation for the catalogues. Damn!" She rolled her eyes and reached behind herself, explaining, "My garters."

Unselfconsciously she hitched her clinging mini skirt over her stocking tops and twisted around to reconnect the garter. On a more voluptuous woman it might have been a distracting sight. On Kylie, the effect was that of a child playing dress-up.

"You kept Ms. Knight's Filofax?" Please goddess, Amanda thought.

Kylie shook her hair extensions. "No. The computer diary. Ms. Knight always copied everything on post-its and stuck them in her Filofax."

"Would you show me?" Amanda could feel her pulse increasing.

Kylie reached happily around the back of the machine and the dull screen fizzed into life. Black nails clattering across the keyboard, she entered the password and flipped her way casually through various menus and files, halting at an image that looked exactly like the page of a day planner.

"It works like this." She showed Amanda how to click back and forth to find different dates and how to view a week at a time. The appointment diary was linked to a data file that contained a list of addresses and phone numbers. Kylie demonstrated this feature like a salesperson, declaring, "Amazingly useful for the busy executive, huh?"

"Brilliant." Amanda felt almost breathless. "That password you used . . ."

"It's Ms. Knight's. You can't get into the system without it. Here —" She scribbled something on a piece of paper. "You'd better have it in case I'm not here later."

Thanking her, Amanda pocketed the password and pulled Sybil's swivel chair into position. A phone was ringing.

"I should get that." Kylie gave a quick apologetic smile and left the room. A moment later, she returned. "It's for you, Inspector. I'll put him through."

Austin Shaw was calling from the hospital. "There's been an accident. It's Marlene Friedman. She's okay."

It had happened just half an hour ago — a hit and run outside the small fruit and vegetable store a few minutes walk from her home. She had been unconscious for a few minutes but was not badly injured. A broken arm. Bruises. Probable concussion.

"Got anything on the driver?" Amanda asked.

"Uniform Branch have a couple of officers at the scene. Someone must have seen the guy."

"Have you spoken to Dr. Friedman?"

"Briefly. She can't remember a thing. She wants to talk to you."

Amanda cast a glance at the computer. "How long before the doctors have finished with her?"

"Probably an hour or so."

"Perfect," Amanda said. "I'll be there."

Sybil's computer diary provided a faithful record of her days. Helpfully it contained the address and telephone details of restaurants she had dined at, friends and professional contacts she had met, and all other appointments she had kept. An entry twelve days before her death listed an appointment with the Carlisle Medical Center, not her usual doctor.

Amanda phoned the number shown and asked to

speak with the Chief Administrator. She was referred to a woman who introduced herself as Mrs. Keats.

Explaining who she was, Amanda said, "I'm calling in connection with a casual patient of yours, Sybil Knight."

The Administrator was instantly solicitous. She had seen last night's news on Channel Two and was horrified.

"I believe Ms. Knight obtained confirmation of a pregnancy at your clinic."

Mrs. Keats paused. She would need to bring up the patient's record on the computer, she said. They had a new system. She commented on the weather and expressed the hope that the killer would be caught. "Aah, here we are," she said. "Yes, it's all here. This is confidential of course."

"All I'm seeking is confirmation of the facts as we know them," Amanda said smoothly.

"Well, she was nine weeks pregnant. She was provided with a referral to Parkview for a termination." The Administrator made a clicking noise with her tongue. "The doctor has added a note about discussing this with her fiance."

"Her fiance attended the appointment?" Amanda felt her hand slipping on the receiver.

"It looks like he phoned later in the day. It happens quite often. The poor things don't know what to do. They have feelings about the baby too, you know."

"And what do you normally say to these unhappy men, Mrs. Keats?"

"It's not appropriate for us to give out details over the phone, so we always encourage them to talk to their partners, Inspector," Mrs. Keats said. "That's what Mr. Jordan was told to do."

"Mr. Jordan?" Amanda said vaguely.

"Ms. Knight's fiance."

CHAPTER SEVENTEEN

Marlene Friedman looked pale and very vulnerable, propped against several pillows, her right arm newly plastered. "I know this sounds ridiculous," she told Amanda. "But I have a feeling I'm being followed. I know I should have said something but I was convinced it was my imagination . . . the stress."

Trying not to convey the increasing sense of urgency she felt, Amanda gave a small sympathetic nod. She had ordered Shaw to bring David Jordan downtown for questioning, and was already mentally preparing for the interview. "Can you tell me what you noticed that might suggest you were being followed," she asked Marlene.

"That's the problem." Marlene's smooth, low voice was tinged with frustration. "There's nothing very tangible. This afternoon, when I left the house, I felt as though someone was watching me."

"You walked to the store?"

"I needed some fresh air."

"What happened?"

Marlene's brow furrowed. "I remember leaving the store and starting to cross the road. You know that wishbone intersection where Maida Vale runs down to the sea . . ."

Amanda nodded. "Some school children reported seeing a car go speeding down there just after you were struck."

"That's all I remember. Just standing there, holding my shopping basket and eating an apple. Then . . . nothing." Marlene seemed disbelieving of her mind's refusal to release the information it must have stored.

"The storekeepers heard squealing tires," Amanda said. "But they didn't get outdoors fast enough to see the car. You were unconscious for several minutes."

"I knew I should have driven." Marlene closed her eyes. "I felt uneasy. And I've been getting phone calls . . . several in the past few days. I answer and it disconnects right away, as if the caller was just finding out if anyone was at home."

"You should have told me."

"It seemed trivial." Absently Marlene explored her plaster with her uninjured hand. "You were investigating Sybil's death, and . . ."

"We hadn't gotten off to such a great start,"

154

Amanda completed with dry humor. "Tell me something, Marlene. Did you ever have this feeling of being watched before Sybil was killed?"

"Not consciously." She hesitated. "On Friday, the day Sybil had her abortion, I felt odd. But I assumed I was reacting to the situation. Sybil was extremely tense, and the clinic itself is such a depressing place."

"You were at the clinic?" Amanda struggled to keep her voice calm. No one at Parkview had said anything about a second person, and she hadn't asked Marlene specifically, so the psychiatrist hadn't told her.

She was losing it, she thought gloomily. Perhaps she was spoiled. As a top homicide detective in underpopulated New Zealand, she was burdened with prestige, a fat pay packet and home and garden, not to mention fawning media attention, enthusiastic subordinates and largely straightforward crimes to solve. Clearly all that success had made her sloppy.

Marlene seemed completely unaware of any problem. "It's a good thing I was with her. There were protesters. I don't know why the police —" She broke off, embarrassed. "I'm sorry. I know it's not your responsibility. But I find those extremists very frightening."

"So do I." Amanda recalled the hatred contorting the faces she had seen that morning. She had finally figured out where she had seen the short man with the bug eyes. His face was in Prostitute's Collective "ugly mugs" file. Amanda couldn't remember what he had done to deserve a listing, but working girls didn't warn each other about dangerous clients without good reason.

"Ironic isn't it," Marlene observed. "They're the

155

very antithesis of what they claim to stand for. We were shouted at and jostled. It was quite appalling. I felt shaken all weekend."

How had Sybil felt? Amanda thought once more about that final diary entry. Clearly her relief at ending the pregnancy had outweighed any trauma involved.

"You're quite certain Kim had no idea about any of this?"

"Sybil said she didn't." There was a note of uncertainty.

It didn't seem a good time to mention that Sybil wasn't exactly glued to the truth. In fact, the more Amanda had learned during the three days the investigation had spanned, the more she suspected Sybil Knight had never told the entire truth about herself to anyone, her therapist included.

"I'm interested in this feeling you've had." Amanda returned to the events of the afternoon. "Tell me more about it."

Marlene rearranged her pillows, wincing a little. "I live alone. The past few nights have been difficult. I lie awake thinking about Sybil. Last night, the neighbor's dog started barking hysterically at three in the morning. I left the lights off and went out into the kitchen. I'm certain I heard my gate click. A few minutes later John came over — that's my neighbor. He was checking to see if I was okay."

"Thoughtful neighbor."

Marlene's smile was a little wry. "I think he was kind of hoping to catch someone. He's the leader of our neighborhood watch group . . . a few of the guys have started some kind of Greypower SWAT team. They call themselves the Roseneath Rangers."

Apparently Marlene found this amusing but also reassuring. "I told John about the gate and he said the Rangers would patrol the house for a few days in case the prowler planned to come back."

"Terrific," Amanda said with an inward sigh. Another bunch of loose cannons taking the law into their own hands. Uniform Branch would be thrilled. "So apart from last night, is there anything else?"

Marlene gave a stilted laugh. "Only paranoia. I'm convinced something bad is going to happen to me."

Creepy phone calls, a late night prowler, a hit-and-run that could be deliberate. "Something bad has already happened," Amanda said. "Do you have any idea what this is about or who could be involved?"

"I don't think I have any enemies."

But Sybil did, and maybe Marlene knew who that person was. "How long have you been seeing David Jordan?" Amanda asked.

"David —" Marlene repeated uncertainly.

"The client you were with when I imposed on you yesterday afternoon."

This earned a mixed response. Marlene was obviously reluctant to discuss a client. She hadn't recognized the name immediately because David Jordan was a new client, she said. Yesterday had been his first appointment.

"When did he contact you?"

"On Wednesday morning." Her tone was repressed.

"Did you know David was a friend of Sybil's?"

"Yes. That's why I agreed to see him immediately. He was terribly distressed about what happened."

"How had he heard about you?"

"Apparently Sybil had suggested he see me."

"Why was that?"

Marlene gave a slightly rueful smile. "Perhaps she thought I was good at my job." Catching Amanda's eye, she made a sheepish gesture, "I'm sorry . . . just trying to lighten up . . . To be honest, I have no idea. Sybil often referred friends to me."

"What was your impression of Mr. Jordan?"

"I barely had time to form one," Marlene replied. "You arrived only a few minutes after he did. He struck me as an introspective person. He was quite tense."

"You made another appointment?"

Marlene shook her head. "He was going overseas. He said he would arrange something when he gets back."

Summoning a professional smile, Amanda asked, "How long are they planning to keep you here?"

"Just for the night," Marlene replied.

"I could assign an officer to the door, if it would make you feel safer."

Marlene's dark eyes crinkled. "I think I've attracted quite enough attention by requesting kosher food and being visited by a brilliant detective."

"Is that a compliment or do you believe everything you read?" Amanda responded lightly.

"If you're asking if I'm impressed or merely impressionable, the answer is yes."

Amanda bent forward, lightly touching Marlene's arm. "Then don't hold out on me, Doctor. If you remember anything else about the accident . . ."

Marlene looked wry. "It was probably a kid in Daddy's sports car."

The casual remark halted Amanda in her tracks.

"I don't know why I said that." Marlene sounded perplexed. "I don't remember the car at all."

But your subconscious does, Amanda thought.

"You think he's our man?" Austin Shaw checked the tape-recorder.

"He's definitely the guy Sybil was seeing." Amanda said. "Whether he killed her is another matter. How did he seem when you picked him up?"

"Twitchy," Shaw replied. "We're lucky to have caught him. The guy is going overseas tonight. His plane leaves at seven."

Amanda glanced at her watch. "I hope he's packed already."

David Jordan stood as they entered the interview room. He was formally dressed, apparently still in his work clothing. One hand fidgeted in the hip pocket of his fine wool jacket, the other smoothed back his sandy-blond hair.

"I'm sorry to disrupt your plans for the afternoon, Mr. Jordan," Amanda said as she and Shaw occupied the two chairs opposite their subject. "I believe DSS Shaw has explained the situation and read your rights. Do you understand that we will be recording this interview?"

"Yes." Sitting down again, David Jordan surveyed her with anxious blue eyes. "Will this take very long? I have to catch a plane tonight."

"I understand you're going on holiday," Amanda said.

"Yes. I have a sister in London."

"Then you must have a lot to do before you

leave. We'll try not to delay you." She placed a thick file of papers on the table and spent a moment leafing through. "Could you describe your relationship with Sybil Knight, Mr. Jordan."

He met her eyes, his demeanor one of earnest cooperation. "We were friends."

"Just friends?"

He hesitated, glancing from her to Shaw. "We were seeing each other," he said quietly.

"You had a sexual relationship?" Amanda asked.

"Yes."

"You were aware that Sybil was in a full-time relationship with Kim Curtis?"

Jordan had the grace to look ashamed. "They were going to break up." His tone was defensive.

"But they didn't, did they Mr. Jordan?" Amanda gave him a hard look and abruptly changed her tone. "Instead Sybil ended your affair. How did you feel about that?"

"Sybil was confused," he said. "She needed some time."

"You thought you could change her mind?" Amanda asked softly. "We know you followed Sybil, Mr. Knight. Why did you do that?"

He stared down at the table. "I don't know what you're talking about."

Amanda watched him for a moment, reading guilt, resentment and denial. "When did you last see Sybil?"

He continued to study the table. "I had lunch with her last Tuesday and I saw her after work on Thursday."

"What did you discuss at lunch?"

He fidgeted. "We just talked. I really don't see what it has to do with you."

"How did you feel about Sybil's pregnancy, Mr. ~~Knight?~~ Jordan?" Amanda asked gently.

His head jerked up and for a split second Amanda caught a glimpse of ferocious anger. "I suppose you know all about it," he said bitterly. "She didn't want the baby. She had her new job and . . . I couldn't make her see sense."

"So what did you do?"

"Do?" His eyes were blank. "What could I do? She had an abortion. She said she never wanted to see me again. I knew it was useless. She wasn't going to change her mind, so I decided to go away for a while. I called my sister and . . ."

"When did you do that," Amanda asked.

He frowned. "About a week ago."

"You must have been very upset," Amanda said.

Jordan glanced at her, as though suspecting insincerity. "The father has no power." His voice was strained.

"You went with Sybil to the Parkview Clinic?" Amanda asked casually.

"No. She didn't want me there."

"Oh . . . I'm sorry," Amanda said in a vague tone. "I naturally assumed —"

"Yes, well you would naturally assume the father would go too." He lifted a shaking hand to brush away a few hairs clinging to his damp forehead. "But she took her therapist, Dr. Friedman."

"I see." Amanda produced a sympathetic look. "How is that for you . . . I mean being one of Dr. Friedman's clients yourself?"

Jordan's body tensed, eyes darting to the file on the table. "I wasn't her client then," he said.

"But you subsequently decided you would start seeing her." Amanda made it very clear she found this inexplicable. "Why?"

He was silent.

"Where were you at midday, today?" Amanda asked.

"Shopping," Jordan said.

"What did you buy, Mr. Jordan?" Austin Shaw took up the questioning, pen poised.

"Nothing," Jordan curtly replied. "I couldn't find what I was looking for."

"Did you know Dr. Friedman was knocked down by a car at lunchtime?" Shaw said. "It was a hit-and-run accident."

Jordan gazed at the floor, his expression screened. "That's dreadful," he mumbled. "Is she all right?"

"She's okay," Amanda responded. "We have a few witnesses, of course. I imagine by the end of the afternoon we will have identified the car."

"What type of car do you own, Mr. Jordan?" Austin Shaw continued his polite questioning.

Jordan was slow to answer, glancing uncertainly from Amanda to Shaw. "A Porsche . . . an old one. Look . . . you can't seriously imagine I had anything to do with it . . . I mean . . . ."

"You were angry with Dr. Friedman, weren't you?" Amanda said. "It's understandable. You're only human."

Jordan wiped at his forehead again. "I don't know what you're talking about."

"Do you deny making phone calls to Dr. Friedman

late at night?" Amanda raised her voice a notch. "Do you deny hanging around her home?"

David Jordan shook his head mechanically.

"I think you saw Dr. Friedman leave her home today and you followed her," Amanda said softly. "Maybe you didn't mean to hit her. Maybe you just wanted to give her a fright. Is that what you wanted, David . . . just to teach her a lesson?"

His gaze swung from the hands clasped in his lap to Amanda's face, its intensity disturbing. "If you think I did it why don't you arrest me." It was somewhere between a taunt and a plea.

Amanda signaled Shaw with a faint nod.

"Please consider your position carefully, Mr. Jordan," he said smoothly. "Hit-and-run is a serious offense. We can understand a driver panicking in the event of an accident, but it is important to come forward."

Quite suddenly Jordan seemed to relax. "Is this going to take much longer?" he inquired.

He knew they were fishing, Amanda thought. It was time to change the subject. "That depends on what you can tell us about Monday night."

"You want to know where I was and what I was doing?" His tone developed a certain jauntiness. "My alibi, right?"

Clearly their subject had rehearsed his story — most people did when they knew they would have to account for their movements. He had worked until eight, he said, then had dinner with a party of Japanese bankers to celebrate a deal. Later in the evening they went to a cabaret. Afterwards, they adjourned to a suite at the Park Royal Hotel and got very drunk. Too intoxicated to get himself home, he'd checked in for the night.

Helpfully, he provided the names of the Japanese visitors and the colleagues present, as well as a copy of his hotel bill, which he just happened to have with him.

"About what time did you go to your room that night?" Austin Shaw asked.

"Around two o'clock."

"And you remained at the hotel for the rest of the night?"

It would be easy to check, Amanda thought. The reception staff would have noticed a guest coming and going in the small hours of the morning.

"I left at eight-thirty," Jordan said. "And went straight to work. I heard about Sybil on Tuesday evening," he added in a hushed tone and cleared his throat, apparently overcome.

"Do you have any idea who might have killed her?" Amanda asked in a businesslike tone.

To her surprise, he came close to smiling. "Perhaps you should ask Kim Curtis. After all, she was the one spying on Sybil. Not me." He directed a swift inquiring glance at Amanda, apparently seeking her response.

"That's very interesting," Amanda said dryly. Getting to her feet, she asked if he had his travel tickets with him.

They were in his briefcase at the front desk, Jordan informed her. She was welcome to take photocopies.

Dispatching Shaw to arrange this, Amanda studied the man opposite her. In sharp contrast to his earlier unease, David Jordan now exuded the calm assurance of a student who had already seen the exam paper. Amanda was aware of an impulse to needle him out of his comfort zone again. "You're going to miss Sybil's funeral," she said in a tone that hinted at how inconsistent this seemed for a person supposedly grief-stricken.

David Jordan met her eyes, his calm unshattered. "I am mourning her in my own way, Inspector."

CHAPTER EIGHTEEN

"Apart from David Jordan, who else owns a sports car?" Amanda stirred some sugar into an insipid Kona coffee.

Most of her team had returned to the inquiry center to file their daily reports. Detectives Bergman and Brody had compiled a list of vehicles registered to the subjects. How did Amanda define a sports car?

"Four wheels and impresses teenage boys," she ventured.

"That's called a hot rod," Brody patiently

informed her. "Kim Curtis owns one of those nifty little Mazdas," she said, leafing through her list. "The model that pretends to be a Lotus. And Jonathan Knight drives a new model Ford Capri."

"Casey Randall?"

"A beat-up Toyota sedan."

Like mine, Amanda silently added.

Everyone else had a family car except for Todd Parker-Brown who drove a tiny yellow Honda hatchback which bore custom plates that read, enigmatically, SCHEMA.

"Sybil's therapist, Dr. Marlene Friedman, was knocked down by a car this afternoon," Amanda said. "She is suffering from a concussion and cannot provide a description of the car or driver. We have a report from two children that a sports car was seen speeding down Maida Vale Road at the time of the accident. They think the color was red."

"Everybody on this list drives a goddamned red car," Bergman muttered.

"That's not entirely surprising." Austin Shaw enlightened the room. "Red is the most popular motor vehicle color in this country. It accounts for nearly two out of three vehicles."

"Kim Curtis's car is green," Brody pointed out.

"Have I missed something, here?" Detective Solomon asked, "Are we still on the Knight homicide or what?"

"In the weeks before she was killed, Sybil Knight was stalked," Amanda said. "We believe David Jordan, the man she had had an affair with, was responsible. But he claims Kim Curtis was following Sybil."

"Like she guessed about the boyfriend?" Nikora said. "Like she was jealous or something?" He looked a little troubled by this concept.

"It's a line we should follow up," Shaw said. "If only to rule out the possibility that Ms. Curtis was involved in the hit-and-run."

"You think this doctor is a target, ma'am?" Nikora started on a new wad of chewing gum. "Like we got some kind of serial thing happening?"

"I'm saying there's a link between Sybil and Dr. Friedman which may have significance for Sybil's killer," Amanda explained.

"So, we stake out the doctor's place . . ." Nikora proposed.

Amanda could see it all too clearly. CIB Homicide setting up shop at Marlene Friedman's home only to find themselves under siege by a bunch of pensioners calling themselves the Roseneath Rangers. She shook her head. "We're putting a guard on her hospital room tonight. Meantime, we've got some work to do to verify David Jordan's story and we don't have a lot of time. He's leaving the country for a month — flying to Auckland tonight and out to London."

"There's about a thousand reporters downstairs," Nikora remarked cheerfully. "Apparently someone's sold their story to the highest bidder. Some chick . . . woman who was with the victim on the night."

"Bernadette Lee," Shaw inserted dryly. "I heard she'll be appearing on *The Debby Daley Hour.*"

"Jordan's alibi for Monday checks out." Austin Shaw stared at his computer screen as he summarized. "The guy worked until eight then had the power dinner with the Japanese bankers. They took in a drag show, and turned up at the Park Royal with several of the dancers. The events created quite an impression on the hotel staff." Shaw passed Amanda a bundle of supporting statements. "Their accounts are very similar."

According to the hotel staff, guests had complained about the noise coming from the Japanese suite and management requested that the visitors leave. Jordan was so intoxicated he checked into a room for the night. A bunch of drag queens had departed at about one-thirty. Shaw had traced two of them so far. They confirmed Jordan's presence at the hotel. Both seemed certain one of their friends had spent the night with him.

"Someone called Paris Latte," Shaw said. "An out-of-towner. I've got Auckland CIB onto it."

Shaw intended to remain at the inquiry center for a while yet. He was analyzing another crop of interviews from the door-to-door. Glancing restlessly about, he said, "Do you have a theory?"

Amanda cradled her head. "I have a headache."

"It's starting to feel like a dead-end case," he said baldly.

Amanda rested the file box against a desk. She knew exactly what he was talking about. All the men in Sybil's life seemed to have strong alibis for Monday night. "We're still waiting on serology," she said. "If those saliva traces came from a woman, we'll try for a match with Kim. No one else has a motive. If she was spying on Sybil she knows a lot more than she's let on."

"Maybe she's not the only possibility. There were

dozens of women at the Lynx that night," Shaw reminded her mildly.

"What are you saying?"

He colored. "I think I'm challenging your objectivity." His gaze was very serious.

Amanda felt winded. She knew Austin Shaw had great professional respect for her. He would not have raised doubts unless he felt the investigation was compromised in some way.

"We've brought two men down here for questioning, but we've soft-gloved the woman Sybil lived with," he said. "We've interviewed virtually every living organism on Harris Street and Civic Square, but we've ignored eighty women who were at the club that night. We took statements from the owner, the bar staff and a few patrons who were there after one. It's not enough. I think we may have missed some important information."

Amanda was silent. It didn't take a cop's instinct to know her colleague was right. Carefully weighing her words, she said, "I'm confident our focus on the people closest to Sybil will lead to the killer."

Shaw looked disbelieving. "Are you telling me the club is off limits?"

Amanda shook her head automatically. What was she saying? That she didn't want male detectives knocking on lesbian doors all over the city, asking questions about their presence at a lesbian club? That she had avoided obtaining a Court order which would compel Casey Randall to hand over a list of club members? It was a classic conflict of interest. She should have put herself off the case. Off the force, maybe.

"I think you're right," she conceded with difficulty. "It's time we got a few people upset."

Austin Shaw was tapping his pen against his keyboard. "In some ways the delay could turn out to be an advantage," he observed. "We know what we're looking for, now. We won't be wasting our time or theirs."

"What do you think we're looking for, Shaw?"

Her colleague examined her steadily. "What if Kim Curtis suspected Sybil of having an affair. What if she decided to catch her and teach her a lesson. Maybe she never meant to kill her."

Amanda could feel denial rising as she confronted the unacceptable idea that a woman could kill the woman she loved. But it happened. Passion had strange bedfellows. Jealousy, irrationality, obsession.

"She doesn't have much of an alibi," Shaw insisted. "She does have a motive. And she's probably the last person Sybil would have suspected."

"She's tiny," Amanda said. "The killer carried Sybil up a flight of stairs."

"Adrenaline," Shaw offered.

"I don't think she's our perpetrator," Amanda said. "But I guess we'd better prove it."

"The Lynx?" Shaw pressed.

"I'm not going in there with a man," Amanda said bluntly. "And I can't see you in a wig and lipstick . . . Call Harrison. Tell her she's in from the cold."

Living down a right of way had its drawbacks.

171

Amanda's neighbors were fighting, a common prelude to the evening meal. He, skinny legs, beer gut over his belt, would arrive home at six and watch the television while she, tortured blonde and blue mascara, fed and bathed their two children. From the kitchen, with her favorite Barry Manilow tape playing, she would yell at him to help her. The children would be screaming. Ignoring them, he would drown out the din by turning up the television.

Tonight their joyous family life was enhanced by the presence of an impressive new motor mower on their front lawn. As Amanda staggered up her steps and struggled to unlock the front door, she heard the wife shout, "It's our fucking anniversary, and you buy a fucking lawn mower. I'm going to kill you!" This was followed by a volley of insults.

Shuddering, Amanda put politically questionable rock music on the stereo and thanked the goddess the worst thing she had to deal with in her personal life was an uppity cat and a best friend who meant well.

She glanced up sharply at the sound of smashing glass. Someone else could call the police, she thought, but all the same listened for any escalation. She was guiltily aware of the small voice that niggled at her each time she heard her neighbors shouting. *It's a domestic. They won't welcome interference.*

She shredded a head of lettuce. Madam was parked in front of her cat bowl, her expression one of bewildered distaste.

"Oh, what's wrong now," Amanda surveyed her. "Is it a cheap cut?"

By way of reply, the diminutive tabby sniffed at

the contents, shook her head as though something grubby had landed on it, and strolled off.

"You're spoiled," Amanda accused. "You've been emotionally blackmailing me ever since I got back here." She pulped an avocado and started chopping onion and tomato. With any luck she would have time for a long bath before she had to meet Harrison.

Humming along with the Rolling Stones, she started up the stairs when there was the blast of an explosion somewhere outside the house, and cursing, she ran for the door.

Her neighbors were standing on their front lawn, the wife holding a petrol canister, the husband frantically wrestling a length of garden hose. Flames engulfed the brand new mower.

Noticing Amanda, the wife shouted, "What's your problem?"

Let them fry, Amanda thought, but, public-spirited, she rushed to help untangle the hose. Water erupted in all directions, the hose snaking away from the husband. As he managed to redirect it onto the conflagration, Amanda said, "Excuse me, I'm a police officer —"

"Oh Christ," the wife snarled. "What next?" Discarding the petrol canister, she stalked past Amanda and disappeared inside the house leaving the husband to vanquish the final flames.

Shaking his head, the guy stared at the charred and dripping mower. "I gave the silly bitch a box of chocolates," he said in an aggrieved tone.

CHAPTER NINETEEN

Harrison was waiting in the inquiry center, her self-consciously injured expression at odds with a flurry of expectant fidgeting.

Amanda greeted her as if their discord did not exist. "How's the Aro Valley, Harrison? Stood on any used hypodermics lately?"

Amanda could almost hear the young woman willing herself not to blush. "We're making progress ma'am. We have several confessions."

"To abduction?"

Harrison shook her head. "Welfare fraud."

She'd changed her hair, Amanda noted. The severe ponytail had been supplanted by an appealing mop of curls.

The missing children were not missing after all, Harrison explained brightly. In fact they had never existed at all. The entire scam had been masterminded by a desperate school board which figured it could increase its funding by adding extra names to the school roll. There were some mothers on welfare who needed extra money . . . So . . .

"They registered the births of non-existent children," Amanda concluded.

"And applied for welfare," Harrison said. "They just borrowed someone else's baby, took it into the Social Welfare Department and said it was born at home. An old guy living behind the launderette forged the doctor's certificates."

"How many children are we talking about?" Amanda wasn't sure she really wanted to know. Already she was mentally assembling the list of charges.

"Thirty maybe," Harrison said.

"That's the equivalent of an entire classroom."

Harrison nodded. "That's what the school needed."

"So DSS Moller has stopped digging up that paddock?"

"Not exactly, ma'am." Harrison shuffled. "Some of the residents want to turn it into a cooperative free range egg farm. They've hired a rotary till machine and since the DSS knows how to drive it . . . Well . . ."

Amanda covered her ears. Joe must have lost his mind. She had seen it coming. The Sauna Strangler Case, which had occurred at a time when his wife Mabel had health problems, had strained their

175

marriage. Since then Joe had become increasingly reluctant to take a role in the most demanding investigations, seeking out desk jobs and lunatic fringe material like the Aro Valley case.

Had he lost his nerve? Was he planning to mark time for the next ten years until he could draw a pension?

"I think it's a good idea to use that land," Harrison declared. "It's only sitting there empty. Why not put it into production?"

"There is the small matter of ownership," Amanda said.

This sentiment was met with disdain. "People are going without food in the Valley and you're worried about some fat cat who wants to build an apartment block that doesn't meet safety standards? I'm starting to think Anya's right — she's the woman who cut my hair — she says the police are pawns of the capitalist patriarchy."

"Fascinating." Amanda handed her impassioned colleague a small paper bag. "Here, have some fries."

"Look at this packaging," Harrison exclaimed. "Did you know that by the year two thousand we won't have any rainforests left? Anya belongs to Greenpeace. She says —"

"Is she cute?" Amanda side-stepped the lecture.

Harrison became so confused she spilled her fries.

Amanda's mouth twitched as she suppressed a grin. "I guess that's a yes."

At ten o'clock the Lynx had barely opened. The music was low and the lighting dim. It was just as well, Amanda thought, steering Harrison toward the bar. The young detective would need a little time to assimilate her surroundings.

Amanda bought her a Coke and reminded her that although they were on duty, for the first hour or so they were simply observing. Just make like the patrons, she advised.

"Which ones?" Harrison glanced nervously about.

A couple of women on the other side of the room blatantly cruised her, one blowing a kiss.

"Relax," Amanda said as a dark-haired woman in severe boy drag approached.

Casey Randall occupied the next barstool and ordered a drink. "I heard you were here." She cast an amused glance at Harrison, adding, "But Alex didn't mention you'd robbed a cradle on the way."

"Detective Harrison was with us on Tuesday," Amanda reminded her.

Casey nodded sagely. "Yes, I remember." She took a slug of her scotch. "Caught your killer yet, Inspector?"

"Not yet," Amanda said. "But I think you can help with that."

"In what way?" Casey's tone was discouraging.

"I need some information from the women who were present earlier on Monday night," Amanda said. "If you could point out your regulars perhaps . . . "

"And what? You're going to question them here?" Casey hissed. "I don't think so."

"I know it's not perfect —" Amanda began.

"Not perfect! It's not happening. Full stop. This is my club. If women can't enjoy themselves in safety here, where can they go?"

Conscious of a hostile stare from the barwoman,

Amanda pasted a sweet smile on her face and said, "You have two choices Casey. You can cooperate, and Harrison and I will conduct our interviews discreetly and tactfully, or you can ask us to leave and we will return sometime in the next few days with twenty uniformed officers who will close you down and escort everyone to the Station."

"That's a threat."

"No," Amanda said mildly. "It's an investigation."

Casey drained her glass. "I don't know how you can compromise yourself like this."

Amanda felt stung. "I believe in what I'm doing, same as you. Someone killed your best friend — right here in your club, where women should be safe. It's my job to find that person."

"And you think it's a lesbian?"

"I can't rule that out without more information," Amanda said.

"Then you'd better talk with Alex." Casey waved the barwoman over. They exchanged a few words, Harrison looking on with comical awe.

"Those tattoos," she mumbled to Amanda. "Are they real?"

At that moment, the subject of her boggling speculation turned, her chill blue eyes sweeping the detectives. When she wasn't serving drinks Alex provided the hired muscle, Amanda figured.

Removing a wad of gum from her mouth, Alex said, "I don't like cops."

It was a promising beginning, Amanda thought dismally.

Over the following hour, as increasing numbers of women entered the room, Alex grudgingly indicated those who had been present the night Sybil was killed. Between times, she bossed the other bar staff around and occasionally chatted up cute, impressionable youngsters.

"You're busy tonight," Amanda remarked to Alex, as she watched Casey Randall escort Harrison from table to table to gather names.

"Payday," Alex explained. "And there's a show coming up."

It was unlikely to be line dancing, Amanda guessed. "A live act?"

"Drag," Alex enlightened her. "The boss goes in for that Queer Nation stuff, so she hired a bunch of queens."

"They perform every night?"

"Mondays, Thursdays and Saturdays."

Amanda felt as if her brain had suddenly kick-started. "What time?"

"Early. They do a few places on the same night. Gotta make a living." Alex's eyes flicked to the door, widening slightly. "Check it out," she muttered.

Following the direction of her gaze, Amanda felt her own jaw dropping.

Standing in the doorway in a leather corset, lace top stockings and stiletto heels, a mini-cam tucked beneath one arm, was Debby Daley. Oblivious of the attention she was attracting, she sashayed to the bar, smiled meltingly at Alex and ordered a glass of Evian water. "Would you mind awfully if I filmed you?" Amanda overheard her inquire girlishly.

Alex looked completely torn. But before she could form a reply, the lights were abruptly dimmed, the music stopped and a spotlight was trained on three spangled queens in lame gowns and opera gloves.

Someone tapped Amanda's arm. "Inspector."

Harrison was at her side, her demeanor agitated. "DSS Shaw called. The serology results came in. We're looking for a man."

"We can arrange the search warrant," Shaw said. "But only God can stop Air New Zealand leaving on time."

Or a crazy, making a bomb threat. Amanda instantly upbraided herself for entertaining the thought. "We don't want to get tangled up in extradition proceedings," she said, checking the time. "The flight departs at twelve-forty, which leaves us precisely twenty minutes. We've got to buy some time."

"They'll be boarding by now," Shaw said.

"Has he cleared Customs yet?"

Harrison shook her head. She was on the phone to the airport, fingers anxiously tapping her desk.

"Auckland CIB owes us a favor or two," Amanda said. Instructing Shaw to complete the formalities for the search warrant, Amanda called their northern counterparts and explained the situation.

"So we arrest the guy? No problem," said the DI on duty.

He sounded vague. In the background Amanda could hear the drone of a television set. The New Zealand rugby side was losing against the Australians. Who could work in the face of this deepening crisis?

"We can't pick him up, yet," she said. "We haven't established sufficient cause."

This didn't seem to worry Auckland. "Mistakes happen," the DI assured her. "Jesus, you wanna work South Auckland, sugar."

Auckland was a sprawling city the same size as Los Angeles but with a lot less people. In recent years the southern suburbs had been afflicted with a pale version of the urban malaise that had transformed South Central L.A. into a battle zone.

"Y'wanna know my theory?" The DI was going to tell her regardless. "If they didn't do it already, they're going to."

"Shoot first and ask questions later, huh?" Amanda said coldly.

He snorted. "If only. This must be the last place on the planet they expect you to go out there unarmed. Two cops wounded last week. We got a fucking war going on and who gives a damn? It's only a fucking cop. We bring the bastards in and what do we get? Some sob story about disadvantaged thirteen-year-olds. Well, we got wives and kids too . . ."

As he continued, Harrison slid a piece of paper in front of Amanda. It read: *Debby Daley is out front asking for you. Are you here?*

Amanda began to shake her head, then, remembering that *The Debby Daley Hour* had bought Bernadette Lee's story, she reconsidered. If there was something Bernadette had chosen not to mention, she wanted to know. Placing her hand over the mouthpiece she instructed Harrison to invite Debby into an interview room.

The embittered Auckland DI was still rambling.

She choked him off briskly, "So you'll call Airport Security and alert them a severe epileptic has boarded without medication."

He got the picture. "We're blue lighting the pills across town in a mercy dash. It's a heart-warming human drama. Effing brilliant."

"Naturally we're not asking them to delay take-off." They wouldn't have to ask, Amanda figured. No airline wants a passenger losing it mid-flight. The bullshit would buy an extra half hour, if they were lucky.

She dropped the phone and strode off toward the interview rooms, conscious of Harrison's troubled stare.

"I have two minutes," she informed Debby Daley, thankful her ex-lover had seen fit to conceal her fetish gear beneath a thick soft wraparound coat.

"I'll be quick, then." Debby gave a brief ironic smile and crossed her legs allowing the coat to fall away. She did nothing to cover the expanse of thigh revealed. "It concerns the story I'm doing on Sybil Knight. A woman called Bernadette Lee has agreed to appear on my show. She was with Sybil on the night she died. I held a preliminary interview with her this afternoon . . ."

Amanda willed herself not to gape at the creamy flesh above Debby's stocking tops. "And?" she prompted impatiently.

"She claims Sybil's partner was at the Lynx that night."

"Really?" Amanda caught a powerful whiff of her scent — Obsession — the fragrance she had always worn when they made love. Very clever, she thought cynically.

"Bernadette said she hadn't told you." There was a hint of pleading in Debby's voice. "I thought it might be important."

"Thanks for letting me know." Amanda got to her feet.

"Is Kim a suspect?" Debby hastily asked.

Amanda shot her a contemptuous look. "There's always a price, isn't there? You're not here to share information, you're fishing for something to hang your damned story on. Debby Daley solves the case before an audience of millions... What's wrong, are your ratings falling?"

In a gesture that was joltingly familiar, Debby bit her bottom lip to stop its trembling. "I wish..." she began hoarsely, then shook her head, murmuring, "Oh, what's the use." Defeatedly, she stood and fastened her coat like a weary child.

Amanda could hardly bear to watch. She knew she was behaving like a complete jerk, yet she couldn't seem to stop herself. It was as though she had to stamp out every spark that remained of her former obsession, for fear it might consume her once more. She had never been able to feel neutral about Debby. Her emotions had always seemed out of control.

Watching Debby reach for the door handle, Amanda's mouth was so dry that she was convinced she would be unable to speak. Before she could prevent herself, she caught Debby's fingers. "I'm sorry," she uttered abruptly.

Standing still, Debby stared, eyes dark with emotion, then she extended a tentative hand to Amanda's face. "I haven't seen anyone else since you," she said softly.

"Don't tell me no one hit on you?" Amanda turned her mouth very deliberately into Debby's palm and kissed it.

At this contact, Debby released a shaky breath and tilting forward, rested her head on Amanda's shoulder. "The two minutes are up," she said.

Amanda slid her arms beneath the heavy coat and drew Debby close. "You smell so good." She grazed Debby's neck with her mouth.

"I want you," Debby whispered, then hastily detached herself at the sound of a sharp knock.

"The car's waiting, Inspector." Janine Harrison stood in the doorway, her gaze averted.

Conscious of an almost overwhelming urge to close the door and pull Debby into her arms, Amanda said, "Thanks Harrison. I'll meet you and the DSS down there in five minutes." As the young detective walked away, she returned her gaze to Debby. "I want you, too," she said.

CHAPTER TWENTY

David Jordan's apartment was only five minutes from the Station, on the fifteenth floor of a converted high rise office building.

The middle-aged security guard seemed unimpressed with the search warrant. Chewing thoughtfully on his gum, he said he'd better call the building supervisor.

"That won't be necessary," Shaw patiently explained. "This is a court order. It means —"

Amanda broke in. "It means you give us the key or we break the door down." Catching Shaw's pained expression, she added for good measure, "It's up to you."

"Was that really necessary?" Shaw muttered as they rode the elevator a moment later.

"You don't go out much, do you Shaw?" Amanda observed.

Harrison, who was staring in embarrassment at her shoes, said in a thin voice. "I thought Jordan had a water-tight alibi."

"We can't verify that until Auckland gets off their butts and finds that queen who shared his room," Amanda said. "Meantime we have conflicting statements. One bellboy claims to have seen her leave the hotel at around one-thirty, a maid says she was definitely in David Jordan's room at seven in the morning."

"In other words there's cause for doubt," Shaw expanded, always keenly aware of his responsibility to train junior staff. "And coupled with the serology report and the evidence about Jordan's close connection to the deceased —"

"We get to invade his privacy." Amanda opened the door with a satisfied flourish and flicked on the lights. The room they entered was spacious and colorless, the walls and furnishings plain.

Harrison stared curiously. "So what exactly are we looking for?"

Amanda walked through the place, getting a general idea of the layout. "We're looking for Sybil Knight's Filofax and her MIL key — it's a flat blue plastic type. Also anything else that connects him to her."

She lifted a framed photograph from the top of a china cabinet. It showed Sybil among a group of people, the photo cropped so that she was in the center.

Leaving Shaw and Harrison to search the living areas, Amanda took the bedroom. The room was tidy to the point of starkness. Starting in the corner nearest the door, she worked her way systematically around the room, removing each drawer from the dresser and carefully rifling the contents, exploring the bedside cabinet, lifting the mattress and the bed base, checking beneath and behind furniture.

David Jordan's wardrobe bore exaggerated testimony to his neatness. His shoes were arranged on several racks, gaps presumably reflecting those chosen to accompany him to England. His suits hung in plastic drycleaning shrouds, his shirts were arranged by color, his ties on a push button conveyor belt.

Amanda grew increasingly pessimistic as she slid the hangers along. A man of Jordan's obsessive neatness would almost certainly have rid himself of any evidence connecting him to a crime.

A series of hat boxes were stacked on the deep shelving above the suits. Collecting a chair from the dining room, Amanda inspected each of them. Nothing.

Harrison appeared in the doorway. "There's a bag in his garbage chute. Shall I get it?"

"Be my guest," Amanda encouraged, putting the hat boxes back again and transferring her attention to a bookshelf choked with Sondra Ray, Buckminster Fuller, the Tao of all manner of things, and the Zen of any subject not covered by these.

Amanda removed everything, pulled the bookcase out and pushed it back into position. From the direction of the kitchen, she could hear dark mutterings, and assumed Harrison was sorting the trash. Shaking each book, she replaced it, then lay on the floor peering again under the furniture and inspecting the carpet for the outline of a floor safe.

Cursing beneath her breath she scrambled up and joined Shaw in the small study. "Zilch," she said.

"Ditto." Shaw looked grim. "I think the guy tidied before he left."

"He's that sort," Amanda agreed. "I'll bet his mother made him clean for his pocket money."

"Mine did," Shaw remarked with a trace of defensiveness. "I think it's valuable training."

"Sure." Amanda nodded as if her mother had given a shit about housework, and the gene had been passed on.

From the kitchen, Harrison yelled, "Hey, I got something."

She was sitting on the floor, surrounded by piles of pungent matter, each diligently arranged on plastic bags. In her lap was a luxuriant blonde wig; in her hand, pieces of a torn photograph.

Amanda laid these out on the bench top, joining them carefully.

"Paris Latte?" Shaw queried.

Amanda shook her head. "David Jordan."

"You're saying he paid Miss Latte to stay the night, then borrowed some of her apparel and walked down to the Lynx?" Shaw asked, a quarter of an hour later at the Station.

"He must have figured Sybil would be there,"

Amanda said. "Apparently she often went on a Monday because it was a quiet night. That way she got to spend some time with Casey. He would have known that from stalking her."

"So he turned up looking like this?" Shaw indicated the photograph.

"It was nearly closing time," Amanda theorized. "He checks out back and sees Sybil's car, so he gains entry. It's easy . . . queens perform at the Lynx, so no one's too surprised to see him. Maybe he says he's lost something or needs to use the bathroom . . . whatever. Then he makes like he's leaving, but instead of going out the front he sneaks back past the staircase and hides himself in the cleaners cupboard. He hears Sybil leave by the front door and figures she's going up to the Gallery for some reason, otherwise she'd have gone out back for her car. Casey locks up. He waits till she's out of the building then he opens the back door, wedges it and waits for Sybil."

"He planned all this ahead of time?" Harrison asked skeptically.

"It's hard to say. I think he planned to go down there and wait for her. I'm still not sure if he planned to kill, but if he did he needed an alibi. Who would connect a queen in a blonde wig with the very drunk David Jordan?"

"So maybe Sybil saw him in the parking lot and didn't recognize him," Harrison ventured. "He pretends his hem is down or his ankle is twisted, maybe. She offers him a ride and he whacks her on the head."

"You got the picture," Amanda said.

"Among the fibers Professor McDougall sampled,

she identified a few strands of synthetic hair," Shaw said. "We may be able to get a match."

Harrison gazed at the torn photograph. "After he did it he went to one of those twenty-four hour booths on the wharf." She sounded appalled. "That's very bizarre. Why would anyone do that?"

"Perhaps it was his way of making the situation real," Amanda reflected.

"It will be real enough when they arrest him at the airport," Harrison said. "When will they send him down?"

"It's too late for a domestic flight tonight. So I'd like you to go up and escort him in the morning."

"Me?" Harrison flushed.

"Any problem with that?"

The young woman was already lifting the phone. "I'll book on the first flight." She gazed solemnly at Amanda. "Should I handcuff myself to the prisoner, ma'am?"

The Auckland CIB finally phoned at one-thirty to confirm that they had arrested David Jordan on suspicion of murder and that he would be detained at Her Majesty's pleasure until Wellington picked him up.

"Grubby little bastard isn't he?" the DI remarked. "Makes you wonder doesn't it, how a loser like him gets to travel business class. Drug money, you can bet your sweet life on that."

Amanda was silent for a long moment. "What did you say?"

The DI started on about the detainee's personal hygiene once more.

Interrupting him, Amanda demanded urgently, "How did you ID this guy?"

"Passport, air ticket, wallet. Course he's denying everything. Probably on drugs." The DI moved right along to the really compelling news — the score for the big game. They'd had a few beers in the canteen, he admitted. Off-duty staff only of course.

"Inspector," Amanda asked with misleading calm, "did you or your staff look at the passport photo?"

There was a predictable silence followed by a predictable defensiveness. "Sure we did. The passport photo was old — he was real clean cut back then . . . probably had a few brain cells left."

Amanda lowered her head to the desk and bumped it several times, as Shaw and Harrison watched with dawning horror.

"Could I speak to the prisoner for a moment, Inspector?"

This was greeted with a lengthy silence, then Amanda heard muffled shouting. "Get that Jordan asshole out to a phone, Sergeant."

A couple of minutes later a voice that differed completely from David Jordan's said, "G'day, this is Brent Campbell speaking. There's been some kind of mistake."

Some guy in a suit had approached Campbell in the mens' room and offered him five hundred notes to swap ID till it was time to collect the luggage at Heathrow. Obviously he wasn't a terrorist or moving drugs or he wouldn't have wanted to pick up his own luggage, Campbell had figured. What kind of idiot would have turned down a business-class ticket plus cash money in exchange for a lousy seat at the back of the plane. He didn't ask too many questions.

The DI came back on the line. "We could book the guy on accessory," he suggested. "And misrepresentation."

"That won't be necessary," Amanda said. "Let's just do our very best to get him on the next plane out of here before he thinks about selling his story to the tabloids."

The DI grunted. "Yeah. Right. No problem, sugar."

"The name's Valentine." Amanda hung up. Asshole, she added silently.

Shaw and Harrison looked like kids whose parents forgot the Christmas presents.

"Go home," Amanda told them. "We've got a funeral to attend tomorrow."

"Yeah," Harrison muttered. "Our own."

"I can't believe we lost him." Inhaling, before she permitted the first rich drop to roll onto her tongue, Amanda sipped the coffee Debby had prepared.

"He's only gone to London," Debby said. "Can't you get him before he checks through Customs?"

"I expect so," Amanda said dully.

"I know it's an anticlimax, but it's quite a story," Debby breathed.

Amanda looked at her sharply, catching a giveaway flash of mischief. "That's not funny."

Debby's smile was provocative. Reaching across, she removed Amanda's cup from her unresisting fingers. "You're scaring me, Inspector," she murmured.

Ditto, Amanda thought, wondering what manner of insanity had prompted her to hand Debby a house key earlier that day. Was she completely spineless?

"Debby," she said awkwardly. "I'm not sure about this."

"You're not sure if you want me, after all?" Debby's bright blue eyes shone with innocent dismay. "Okay." She got to her feet. "I guess what you really need is a nice hot shower, some sleep, some privacy . . . Right?"

Amanda contemplated the delicate arch of Debby's neck, the welcoming fullness of her mouth. "Wrong," she croaked. "I need . . ." She couldn't continue. Her throat felt raw, desire clenched her stomach.

Moving to Debby, she arrested the hands that were buttoning her jacket, sensing in Debby's slight shiver an apprehension that matched her own. She brushed Debby's mouth lightly with a fingertip and murmured, "Let's not talk right now."

Debby met her eyes, and freeing her hands, placed them on either side of Amanda's face. Very deliberately she kissed her, first on the cheeks then the mouth. "Promise me one thing," she said gravely. "Don't regret this. Not tomorrow. Not ever."

Amanda lowered her head to Debby's breasts. Listening to her steady heart, she whispered, "I promise."

CHAPTER TWENTY-ONE

Amanda awoke late and stared with faint shock at the woman in her bed. Resisting the urge to wake her, she crept out of the room and into the kitchen.

Madam wound herself soundlessly around her ankles, her small warm body vibrating with pleasure.

"I feel that way about hamburger, too," Amanda said, scooping food into the cat bowl.

As Madam ate, Amanda made coffee and listened to her messages. There were two days' worth. Roseanne reminding her that they were going skiing in a week's time, the delicatessen confirming her coffee delivery, her mother calling from New Jersey to say that she was dating a guy who channeled JFK, Austin Shaw ringing to say he had some information.

Amanda called him. "I thought you were off-duty today."

"Someone has to deal with the media. The Chief was on the phone at six this morning. Sir George got to hear about that Lee woman going on *The Debby Daley Hour*. He wants you to use your persuasive powers to stop her running the show."

"Fat chance," Amanda said.

Shaw sighed. "It gets worse. We seem to have another complication. About an hour ago Brett Campbell's passport and air ticket were found in a rubbish bin in the Auckland airport bar along with Sybil Knight's Filofax and MIL key."

Amanda rubbed the remaining sleep out of her eyes.

"It seems possible that he may have had a false passport all the time and simply planned the switch to throw us off the trail," Shaw said.

"You've talked to Scotland Yard?"

"We sent a graphic on-line. They'll intercept him at Customs, whatever name he's under. We'll get him in the end."

Amanda frowned. "You're certain he was on that plane?" This wasn't *Mission Impossible*. Fake passports might be a dime a dozen on TV thrillers but even professional criminals had difficulty laying their hands on one in New Zealand. Maybe Jordan had taken fright once he'd done the swap with Brent Campbell. Maybe he had abandoned the whole idea of leaving the country.

Amanda suggested this to Shaw, who said he had

already arranged a stake-out at Jordan's apartment. There was no sign of the guy. He would get down there himself, he said.

Agreeing, Amanda hung up. She buttered a bagel and carried this to the table with a plunger of coffee. What the hell was David Jordan up to? It was ten o'clock. If he had returned to Wellington, he could have arrived on the seven-thirty flight. If he wasn't at his apartment, where was he?

Frowning, she laced her Nikes, buckled her holster and checked that her Smith & Wesson was loaded.

"What are you doing?" Debby was framed in the door, blinking sleepily.

"I have to go out," Amanda said. She could almost feel herself becoming defensive.

"Me too." Debby sauntered nonchalantly across the room and planted a lingering kiss on her mouth. "I'd give you a ride, but I have to pick up my crew."

Amanda stared for a moment then started to laugh.

"Did I miss something," Debby asked.

"No." Amanda kissed her back. "I did." She pulled on her jacket and headed for the door.

Debby waved cheerfully. "I'll see you at the funeral."

Amanda got to the hospital a few minutes after the time she had arranged to collect Marlene.

"She's just gone," the charge nurse said. "She didn't want to bother you. So she took a cab."

Amanda jogged back to her car. It would be fine,

she thought as she drove out the hospital gates. David Jordan was probably somewhere in Auckland, lying low until the heat died down, or else he was on that plane under some other name, blithely unaware that Scotland Yard would be waiting for him at the other end.

She applied her foot to the accelerator. Was it possible that David had attacked Marlene simply because he suspected her of knowing his identity? It seemed unlikely. It was the abortion, Amanda thought. He probably held Marlene to blame in some way and thought she should be punished too.

It didn't take Einstein to figure that out, but it was so obvious and so irrational that she had trouble believing it could be a motive for attempted murder.

She swung hard around the hairpin corners on Roseneath hill and found a place to park a few doors from Marlene's house. A taxi was just leaving.

Unbuttoning her jacket, Amanda approached the gate opening it very carefully. Marlene's front door was open and her bags were sitting on the doorstep.

Amanda waited a moment then soft-shoed down the path to the door and slid quietly inside. She could hear voices coming from the living area, the man's insistent, the woman's calm. Padding along the hallway, she drew the .357, and, bracing it across her left arm, ducked inside Marlene's sitting room in time to hear David Jordan explain that he really had no choice. Sybil and Marlene had conspired to kill his child and they would have to pay.

Marlene's feet were tied to her good arm. Watching her from across his shoulder, Jordan was tapping out one of her tall windows with a poker.

"I didn't intend to kill her," Jordan said. "Murder

is very bad karma. It must have been her time. A life for a life."

"It's not my time, David," Marlene said. "If you take my life you must accept the consequences in this life and in those that follow."

"I'm not going to kill you either, Doctor." Jordan sounded slightly indignant. "You'll be taking your chances with fate. It's quite a way down from here, but you may land in a tree. Or you may go all the way to the rocks. Karma will dictate."

"I don't think so," Amanda said loudly. Training her gun on him, she said, "Freeze. Drop the poker and lift your hands above your head. Marlene, shift yourself toward me."

With a peculiar smile, Jordan threw the poker with full force at Amanda. Dodging it, she plunged toward him, her hands grasping air as he leapt from the window.

Amanda stared down after him, sickened. His body lay like a bundle of rags on the rocks below. Bracing herself against the window frame, she turned to Marlene. "Are you all right?"

"I think so. Thank you."

As Amanda untied her, Marlene took a deep breath, and a small amount of color entered her cheeks.

"You should have waited at the hospital for me," Amanda said.

The psychiatrist nodded absently. "Then he would have died alone." At Amanda's frown, she said, "He wanted company. So he thought he would take me along. If you hadn't insisted on seeing me the day he was here, he'd have killed me then."

He had never intended to go to England, Amanda

thought. And a passport was not necessary for the destination he was headed for. It made sense, she supposed. For a mad person.

CHAPTER TWENTY-TWO

Like most weddings and funerals, Sybil Knight's
had brought together an ill-matched assortment of
people. For a split second Amanda permitted herself
to remember her own impassivity at Kelly's funeral
seven years ago. Utterly preoccupied with the swirling
grain of the wooden pew beneath her fingers, and the
way dust had floated on shafts of light from the
stained-glass windows high above, she wouldn't have
noticed a bomb going off. She wondered if she would
ever feel anything but numb rage at the death of the
woman she had loved.

Amanda studied the crowd gathered outside the cathedral, guessing at the identities of various contingents — well heeled relatives, friends of the victim, friends of the victim's partner, work and business acquaintances. Almost everybody looked awkward, except perhaps Casey Randall, who looked shamelessly sexy.

Debby was positioned behind the media cordon. Amanda could barely look at her without her flesh quivering. Debby seemed to be having the same problem, dropping her microphone the last time they had exchanged a glance.

Harrison treated Amanda to a look of abject suspicion. "Ma'am," she said in a stage-whisper. "I know your private life is off-limits, but are you seeing that reporter?"

Amanda winced. "You know I can't answer that, but if I could, I'd say maybe."

"I knew it," Harrison said. "You're wearing odd socks today."

Amanda stared at her feet. Sure enough one sock was gray, the other navy to match her uniform. She could feel herself blushing.

People were entering the church and filing past Sybil's coffin. Amanda absently followed, glad to leave the chill of the overcast outdoors. Passing the front pew she saw Kim Curtis sitting with the Knights and felt a sharp sorrow that Kim had learned more about her lover in death than she had in life.

Sybil lay in her coffin like a doll in a gift box, a mask of heavy make-up concealing her bruising. With curious detachment, Amanda stared down at her, and wondered, as she always did, whether fate was random and if life had any purpose at all. In that single moment shared with the dead, she found herself intensely grateful to be alive. Glancing back into the crowd she spotted Debby directing her camera crew, and smiled.

Maybe she was seeing that reporter. It was enough.

A few of the publications of
THE NAIAD PRESS, INC.
P.O. Box 10543 • **Tallahassee, Florida 32302**
Phone (904) 539-5965
Toll-Free Order Number: 1-800-533-1973
Mail orders welcome. Please include 15% postage.

SECOND GUESS by Rose Beecham. 216 pp. An Amanda Valentine
Mystery. 2nd in a series.   ISBN 1-56280-069-8 $9.95

THE SURE THING by Melissa Hartman. 208 pp. L.A. earthquake
romance.   ISBN 1-56280-078-7   9.95

A RAGE OF MAIDENS by Lauren Wright Douglas. 240 pp. A
Caitlin Reece Mystery. 6th in a series.   ISBN 1-56280-068-X   9.95

TRIPLE EXPOSURE by Jackie Calhoun. 224 pp. Romantic drama
involving many characters.   ISBN 1-56280-067-1   9.95

UP, UP AND AWAY by Catherine Ennis. 192 pp. Delightful
romance.   ISBN 1-56280-065-5   9.95

PERSONAL ADS by Robbi Sommers. 176 pp. Sizzling short
stories.   ISBN 1-56280-059-0   9.95

FLASHPOINT by Katherine V. Forrest. 256 pp. Lesbian
blockbuster!   ISBN 1-56280-043-4   22.95

CROSSWORDS by Penny Sumner. 256 pp. 2nd Victoria Cross
Mystery.   ISBN 1-56280-064-7   9.95

SWEET CHERRY WINE by Carol Schmidt. 224 pp. A novel of
suspense.   ISBN 1-56280-063-9   9.95

CERTAIN SMILES by Dorothy Tell. 160 pp. Erotic short stories.
                                             ISBN 1-56280-066-3   9.95

EDITED OUT by Lisa Haddock. 224 pp. 1st Carmen Ramirez
Mystery.   ISBN 1-56280-077-9   9.95

WEDNESDAY NIGHTS by Camarin Grae. 288 pp. Sexy
adventure.   ISBN 1-56280-060-4   10.95

SMOKEY O by Celia Cohen. 176 pp. Relationships on the playing
field.   ISBN 1-56280-057-4   9.95

KATHLEEN O'DONALD by Penny Hayes. 256 pp. Rose and
Kathleen find each other and employment in 1909 NYC.
                                             ISBN 1-56280-070-1   9.95

STAYING HOME by Elisabeth Nonas. 256 pp. Molly and Alix
want a baby . . . or do they?   ISBN 1-56280-076-0   10.95

TRUE LOVE by Jennifer Fulton. 240 pp. Six lesbians searching for
love in all the "right" places.   ISBN 1-56280-035-3   9.95

GARDENIAS WHERE THERE ARE NONE by Molleen Zanger.
176 pp. Why is Melanie inextricably drawn to the old house?
                                                   ISBN 1-56280-056-6   9.95

MICHAELA by Sarah Aldridge. 256 pp. A "Sarah Aldridge"
romance.   ISBN 1-56280-055-8   10.95

KEEPING SECRETS by Penny Mickelbury. 208 pp. A Gianna
Maglione Mystery. First in a series.   ISBN 1-56280-052-3   9.95

THE ROMANTIC NAIAD edited by Katherine V. Forrest &
Barbara Grier. 336 pp. Love stories by Naiad Press authors.
                                                   ISBN 1-56280-054-X   14.95

UNDER MY SKIN by Jaye Maiman. 336 pp. A Robin Miller
mystery. 3rd in a series.   ISBN 1-56280-049-3.   10.95

STAY TOONED by Rhonda Dicksion. 144 pp. Cartoons — 1st
collection since Lesbian Survival Manual.   ISBN 1-56280-045-0   9.95

CAR POOL by Karin Kallmaker. 272pp. Lesbians on wheels
and then some!   ISBN 1-56280-048-5   9.95

NOT TELLING MOTHER: STORIES FROM A LIFE by Diane
Salvatore. 176 pp. Her 3rd novel.   ISBN 1-56280-044-2   9.95

GOBLIN MARKET by Lauren Wright Douglas. 240pp. A Caitlin
Reece Mystery. 5th in a series.   ISBN 1-56280-047-7   9.95

LONG GOODBYES by Nikki Baker. 256 pp. A Virginia Kelly
mystery. 3rd in a series.   ISBN 1-56280-042-6   9.95

FRIENDS AND LOVERS by Jackie Calhoun. 224 pp. Mid-western
Lesbian lives and loves.   ISBN 1-56280-041-8   9.95

THE CAT CAME BACK by Hilary Mullins. 208 pp. Highly praised
Lesbian novel.   ISBN 1-56280-040-X   9.95

BEHIND CLOSED DOORS by Robbi Sommers. 192 pp. Hot, erotic
short stories.   ISBN 1-56280-039-6   9.95

CLAIRE OF THE MOON by Nicole Conn. 192 pp. See the movie —
read the book!   ISBN 1-56280-038-8   10.95

SILENT HEART by Claire McNab. 192 pp. Exotic Lesbian
romance.   ISBN 1-56280-036-1   9.95

HAPPY ENDINGS by Kate Brandt. 272 pp. Intimate conversations
with Lesbian authors.   ISBN 1-56280-050-7   10.95

THE SPY IN QUESTION by Amanda Kyle Williams. 256 pp. 4th
Madison McGuire.   ISBN 1-56280-037-X   9.95

SAVING GRACE by Jennifer Fulton. 240 pp. Adventure and
romantic entanglement.   ISBN 1-56280-051-5   9.95

THE YEAR SEVEN by Molleen Zanger. 208 pp. Women surviving
in a new world.   ISBN 1-56280-034-5   9.95

CURIOUS WINE by Katherine V. Forrest. 176 pp. Tenth
Anniversary Edition. The most popular contemporary Lesbian
love story.   ISBN 1-56280-053-1   10.95

CHAUTAUQUA by Catherine Ennis. 192 pp. Exciting, romantic
adventure.   ISBN 1-56280-032-9   9.95

A PROPER BURIAL by Pat Welch. 192 pp. A Helen Black
mystery. 3rd in a series.   ISBN 1-56280-033-7   9.95

SILVERLAKE HEAT: A Novel of Suspense by Carol Schmidt.
240 pp. Rhonda is as hot as Laney's dreams.   ISBN 1-56280-031-0   9.95

LOVE, ZENA BETH by Diane Salvatore. 224 pp. The most talked
about lesbian novel of the nineties!   ISBN 1-56280-030-2   9.95

A DOORYARD FULL OF FLOWERS by Isabel Miller. 160 pp.
Stories incl. 2 sequels to *Patience and Sarah.*   ISBN 1-56280-029-9   9.95

MURDER BY TRADITION by Katherine V. Forrest. 288 pp. A
Kate Delafield Mystery. 4th in a series.   ISBN 1-56280-002-7   9.95

THE EROTIC NAIAD edited by Katherine V. Forrest & Barbara Grier.
224 pp. Love stories by Naiad Press authors.   ISBN 1-56280-026-4   12.95

DEAD CERTAIN by Claire McNab. 224 pp. A Carol Ashton
mystery. 5th in a series.   ISBN 1-56280-027-2   9.95

CRAZY FOR LOVING by Jaye Maiman. 320 pp. A Robin Miller
mystery. 2nd in a series.   ISBN 1-56280-025-6   9.95

STONEHURST by Barbara Johnson. 176 pp. Passionate regency
romance.   ISBN 1-56280-024-8   9.95

INTRODUCING AMANDA VALENTINE by Rose Beecham.
256 pp. An Amanda Valentine Mystery. First in a series.
                                               ISBN 1-56280-021-3   9.95

UNCERTAIN COMPANIONS by Robbi Sommers. 204 pp.
Steamy, erotic novel.   ISBN 1-56280-017-5   9.95

A TIGER'S HEART by Lauren W. Douglas. 240 pp. A Caitlin
Reece mystery. 4th in a series.   ISBN 1-56280-018-3   9.95

PAPERBACK ROMANCE by Karin Kallmaker. 256 pp. A
delicious romance.   ISBN 1-56280-019-1   9.95

MORTON RIVER VALLEY by Lee Lynch. 304 pp. Lee Lynch at
her best!   ISBN 1-56280-016-7   9.95

THE LAVENDER HOUSE MURDER by Nikki Baker. 224 pp. A
Virginia Kelly Mystery. 2nd in a series.   ISBN 1-56280-012-4   9.95

PASSION BAY by Jennifer Fulton. 224 pp. Passionate romance,
virgin beaches, tropical skies.   ISBN 1-56280-028-0   9.95

STICKS AND STONES by Jackie Calhoun. 208 pp. Contemporary
lesbian lives and loves. ISBN 1-56280-020-5 9.95

DELIA IRONFOOT by Jeane Harris. 192 pp. Adventure for Delia
and Beth in the Utah mountains. ISBN 1-56280-014-0 9.95

UNDER THE SOUTHERN CROSS by Claire McNab. 192 pp.
Romantic nights Down Under. ISBN 1-56280-011-6 9.95

RIVERFINGER WOMEN by Elana Nachman/Dykewomon.
208 pp. Classic Lesbian/feminist novel. ISBN 1-56280-013-2 8.95

GRASSY FLATS by Penny Hayes. 256 pp. Lesbian romance in
the '30s. ISBN 1-56280-010-8 9.95

A SINGULAR SPY by Amanda K. Williams. 192 pp. 3rd Madison
McGuire. ISBN 1-56280-008-6 8.95

THE END OF APRIL by Penny Sumner. 240 pp. A Victoria Cross
Mystery. First in a series. ISBN 1-56280-007-8 8.95

A FLIGHT OF ANGELS by Sarah Aldridge. 240 pp. Romance set at
the National Gallery of Art ISBN 1-56280-001-9 9.95

HOUSTON TOWN by Deborah Powell. 208 pp. A Hollis Carpenter
mystery. Second in a series. ISBN 1-56280-006-X 8.95

KISS AND TELL by Robbi Sommers. 192 pp. Scorching stories by
the author of *Pleasures*. ISBN 1-56280-005-1 9.95

STILL WATERS by Pat Welch. 208 pp. A Helen Black mystery.
2nd in a series. ISBN 0-941483-97-5 9.95

TO LOVE AGAIN by Evelyn Kennedy. 208 pp. Wildly
romantic love story. ISBN 0-941483-85-1 9.95

IN THE GAME by Nikki Baker. 192 pp. A Virginia Kelly
mystery. First in a series. ISBN 1-56280-004-3 9.95

AVALON by Mary Jane Jones. 256 pp. A Lesbian Arthurian
romance. ISBN 0-941483-96-7 9.95

STRANDED by Camarin Grae. 320 pp. Entertaining, riveting
adventure. ISBN 0-941483-99-1 9.95

THE DAUGHTERS OF ARTEMIS by Lauren Wright Douglas.
240 pp. A Caitlin Reece mystery. 3rd in a series.
ISBN 0-941483-95-9 9.95

CLEARWATER by Catherine Ennis. 176 pp. Romantic secrets
of a small Louisiana town. ISBN 0-941483-65-7 8.95

THE HALLELUJAH MURDERS by Dorothy Tell. 176 pp. A Poppy
Dillworth mystery. 2nd in a series. ISBN 0-941483-88-6 8.95

SECOND CHANCE by Jackie Calhoun. 256 pp. Contemporary
Lesbian lives and loves. ISBN 0-941483-93-2 9.95

BENEDICTION by Diane Salvatore. 272 pp. Striking,
contemporary romantic novel. ISBN 0-941483-90-8 9.95

BLACK IRIS by Jeane Harris. 192 pp. Caroline's hidden past . . .
ISBN 0-941483-68-1   8.95

TOUCHWOOD by Karin Kallmaker. 240 pp. Loving, May/
December romance.   ISBN 0-941483-76-2   9.95

COP OUT by Claire McNab. 208 pp. A Carol Ashton mystery.
4th in a series.   ISBN 0-941483-84-3   9.95

THE BEVERLY MALIBU by Katherine V. Forrest. 288 pp. A
Kate Delafield Mystery. 3rd in a series.   ISBN 0-941483-48-7   9.95

THAT OLD STUDEBAKER by Lee Lynch. 272 pp. Andy's affair
with Regina and her attachment to her beloved car.
ISBN 0-941483-82-7   9.95

PASSION'S LEGACY by Lori Paige. 224 pp. Sarah is swept into
the arms of Augusta Pym in this delightful historical romance.
ISBN 0-941483-81-9   8.95

THE PROVIDENCE FILE by Amanda Kyle Williams. 256 pp.
Second Madison McGuire   ISBN 0-941483-92-4   8.95

I LEFT MY HEART by Jaye Maiman. 320 pp. A Robin Miller
Mystery. First in a series.   ISBN 0-941483-72-X   9.95

THE PRICE OF SALT by Patricia Highsmith (writing as Claire
Morgan). 288 pp. Classic lesbian novel, first issued in 1952 . . .
acknowledged by its author under her own, very famous, name.
ISBN 1-56280-003-5   9.95

SIDE BY SIDE by Isabel Miller. 256 pp. From beloved author of
Patience and Sarah.   ISBN 0-941483-77-0   9.95

STAYING POWER: LONG TERM LESBIAN COUPLES
by Susan E. Johnson. 352 pp. Joys of coupledom.
ISBN 0-941-483-75-4   12.95

SLICK by Camarin Grae. 304 pp. Exotic, erotic adventure.
ISBN 0-941483-74-6   9.95

NINTH LIFE by Lauren Wright Douglas. 256 pp. A Caitlin
Reece mystery. 2nd in a series.   ISBN 0-941483-50-9   8.95

PLAYERS by Robbi Sommers. 192 pp. Sizzling, erotic novel.
ISBN 0-941483-73-8   9.95

MURDER AT RED ROOK RANCH by Dorothy Tell. 224 pp.
A Poppy Dillworth mystery. 1st in a series.   ISBN 0-941483-80-0   8.95

LESBIAN SURVIVAL MANUAL by Rhonda Dicksion.
112 pp. Cartoons!   ISBN 0-941483-71-1   8.95

A ROOM FULL OF WOMEN by Elisabeth Nonas. 256 pp.
Contemporary Lesbian lives.   ISBN 0-941483-69-X   9.95

THEME FOR DIVERSE INSTRUMENTS by Jane Rule. 208
pp. Powerful romantic lesbian stories.   ISBN 0-941483-63-0   8.95

LESBIAN QUERIES by Hertz & Ertman. 112 pp. The questions
you were too embarrassed to ask.   ISBN 0-941483-67-3   8.95

CLUB 12 by Amanda Kyle Williams. 288 pp. Espionage thriller
featuring a lesbian agent!   ISBN 0-941483-64-9   8.95

DEATH DOWN UNDER by Claire McNab. 240 pp. A Carol
Ashton mystery. 3rd in a series.   ISBN 0-941483-39-8   9.95

MONTANA FEATHERS by Penny Hayes. 256 pp. Vivian and
Elizabeth find love in frontier Montana. ISBN 0-941483-61-4   8.95

LIFESTYLES by Jackie Calhoun. 224 pp. Contemporary Lesbian
lives and loves.   ISBN 0-941483-57-6   9.95

WILDERNESS TREK by Dorothy Tell. 192 pp. Six women on
vacation learning "new" skills.   ISBN 0-941483-60-6   8.95

MURDER BY THE BOOK by Pat Welch. 256 pp. A Helen
Black Mystery. First in a series.   ISBN 0-941483-59-2   9.95

THERE'S SOMETHING I'VE BEEN MEANING TO TELL
YOU Ed. by Loralee MacPike. 288 pp. Gay men and lesbians
coming out to their children.   ISBN 0-941483-44-4   9.95

LIFTING BELLY by Gertrude Stein. Ed. by Rebecca Mark. 104
pp. Erotic poetry.   ISBN 0-941483-51-7   8.95

AFTER THE FIRE by Jane Rule. 256 pp. Warm, human novel
by this incomparable author.   ISBN 0-941483-45-2   8.95

THREE WOMEN by March Hastings. 232 pp. Golden oldie. A
triangle among wealthy sophisticates.   ISBN 0-941483-43-6   8.95

PLEASURES by Robbi Sommers. 204 pp. Unprecedented
eroticism.   ISBN 0-941483-49-5   8.95

EDGEWISE by Camarin Grae. 372 pp. Spellbinding
adventure.   ISBN 0-941483-19-3   9.95

FATAL REUNION by Claire McNab. 224 pp. A Carol Ashton
mystery. 2nd in a series.   ISBN 0-941483-40-1   8.95

KEEP TO ME STRANGER by Sarah Aldridge. 372 pp. Romance
set in a department store dynasty.   ISBN 0-941483-38-X   9.95

IN EVERY PORT by Karin Kallmaker. 228 pp. Jessica's sexy,
adventuresome travels.   ISBN 0-941483-37-7   9.95

OF LOVE AND GLORY by Evelyn Kennedy. 192 pp. Exciting
WWII romance.   ISBN 0-941483-32-0   8.95

CLICKING STONES by Nancy Tyler Glenn. 288 pp. Love
transcending time.   ISBN 0-941483-31-2   9.95

These are just a few of the many Naiad Press titles — we are the oldest and
largest lesbian/feminist publishing company in the world. Please request a
complete catalog. We offer personal service; we encourage and welcome
direct mail orders from individuals who have limited access to bookstores
carrying our publications.